love will save your soul

KATRINA MARIE

Boy Child & Wee One, both of you inspire me daily. Never lose sight of your goals.

SLIVERS OF MOONLIGHT filter in through the blinds, illuminating the otherwise dark room. Dawson lies next to me, snoring softly. This is something I would have found adorable when we started dating. Now, it's annoying that he can sleep peacefully. He should be the one wide awake, in turmoil over the words he's thrown at me.

Instead, I'm the one curled up into a ball wondering how the hell I got here. It's not how I envisioned our lives together. When we first moved in together, everything was *perfect*. We spent time together every night, and I knew he adored me. Now... now, I'm always waiting for the other shoe to drop. Never knowing when something I say is going to set him off. Every day is like walking on eggshells, hoping he'll be in a good mood.

If my parents knew how badly my relationship has gone downhill, they would be appalled. Dawson has never laid a hand on me, but the verbal slams pain me almost as much. A shard of glass, glinting in the corner, catches my eye. It's a small reminder of pissing him off earlier this evening because I didn't fold his laundry the way he likes it. The vase hitting the wall before shattering will forever be etched into my mind. I should be used to it by now, the sound of whatever he can get his hands on hitting the wall. But it's not something I should ever have to be accustomed to.

Everyone has an opinion about how they would react if they found themselves in this sort of situation. They will never truly know the fear that courses through you at the thought of leaving. The lengths a person like Dawson will go through in order to keep you by their side. The *I'm sorry's*, and empty promises. All of it grooming you, cultivating you to do what you're *supposed* to do, and stand beside them. Even when the very sight of them makes you sick to your stomach.

But no more. At least, not for me. I'm done being the person he takes out his anger on. No longer willing to be the one he uses to make himself feel big. I am better than this. I *deserve* more than this.

With one last glance at Dawson's sleeping form, I gently climb out of bed. The bags I packed hours before he got home await me in the coat closet. Most would call me a coward for taking off in the middle of the night, but it's the only time I can ensure that I'm going to get out with my dignity intact.

As quietly as possible, I pull my bags out of the closet

and my keys off the key hook. Opening the door, I breathe in the cold winter night. My first taste of freedom in over six months. A voice from down the hallway stops me in my tracks.

"Going somewhere?" Dawson asks, voice scratchy with sleep.

Part of me wants to turn around and put my bags up. To beg for forgiveness and hope this isn't the time he'll begin using his fists. But I push that reaction down, determined to take my stand and be the strong person I know is hidden deep inside me. "Yeah," my voice comes out in a squeak. Clearing my throat, I try again. "Yes, I'm going to my parents."

"No, you aren't," he takes a step toward me, hands curled into fists at his side.

The urge to retreat courses through me. Dropping my bags and running for my car would be the easiest option. But... it could also end with me stumbling over something and hurting myself in the process. If I don't stand up for myself now, there's no guarantee I won't come back to him later. It's a vicious cycle, and one that I'm sick of. Straightening my back, I broaden my shoulders. I *refuse* to let him intimidate me the way he has. Refuse to let him think he can control me for one second longer. "Yes, I am," I lift my chin higher. "I'm done, Dawson. This isn't working for me. The yelling, throwing things at me... I deserve more than that. You aren't the man I thought you were when we first moved in together. I won't be your prisoner anymore."

Tightening my grip on my keys in one hand, and my bag in the other, I step outside the door. This place is no longer my home. "Goodbye, Dawson."

"You can't just leave me, Sophie." His voice is pained. "I'll do better. Go to counseling. Anything." The sad thing is, I've heard all this before. Things will be great between us for a week or two, then it's back to the same old story.

"Sorry," I close the door behind me and walk briskly to my car. Fear makes me want to look back, but I don't. He's not going to follow me. Not yet, anyway. I'm sure he'll show up at my parents' house with some sob story. But by then, it'll be too late. They'll know the truth of how my life has been. There's no way Mom, or Dad, will let him come anywhere near me.

Unlocking my car door, I throw my bags into the passenger seat before sliding behind the wheel. A glance toward the apartment shows Dawson's shadowed outline in the doorway. Without taking my eyes off the door, I start the car and put it in gear. It's time to rebuild myself and put everything Dawson tore down back together.

sophia

IT'S BEEN four months since I walked out of the apartment I shared with Dawson. My parents reacted exactly the way I thought they were going to when I showed up on their doorstep in the middle of the night. They were upset I didn't say anything to them sooner, but mostly they were happy I was okay. That I finally got myself out of a bad situation they hadn't realize existed.

Mom and Dad have done an amazing job of keeping Dawson away from me, too. Any other guy would have run screaming with the threats Dad threw at him. Not him, though. He took it as a challenge to see how long it would take before he could persuade my parents into letting him see me. That is until we took out a restraining order against him. He hasn't shown up since.

Before we got that taken care of, I was terrified to leave the house. Always worried Dawson was going to jump out from behind a row of bushes. While I'd like to say that I don't feel any fear when I leave the house, that would be a lie. Constantly looking over my shoulder is something I think I'm going to do for a long time, if not forever. I want to believe he'd never physically hurt me, but I'm not sure of that. His temper kept getting worse and worse. How do I know that he wouldn't have taken it a step further? That thought alone is what scares me more than anything.

"Sophie," Mom yells from the living room, pulling my thoughts away from Dawson and all that he has done. She acts as if I can't hear her at a normal level from the kitchen. We are maybe twenty feet away from each other.

"Yeah, Mom." My fingers are poised over my laptop keyboard, filling out yet another job application. It would be amazing if one of them actually responded, or even gave me a "no, thank you." Not hearing anything is driving me batty.

"How's the search going?"

She asks me this at least twice a day. As if I'm lazing about not trying to find another way to replace my income. When fear kept me from leaving my parents' house, my job was understanding… at first. When there were consecutive days missed, thanks to Dawson's harassment, they made the decision to let me go indefinitely. There's a tiny part of me that hoped they would give me another chance, but it's not something they were comfortable doing. I can't blame them, not really. It's not their fault I decided to date a controlling, overbearing asshole. Maybe if I'm quiet long enough she'll forget she asked.

Minutes pass without another sound from the living room, and I breathe a sigh of relief. My fingers ache from the constant scrolling as job listings pop up on the screen. My qualifications do not fit any of these jobs. Most require a degree that I don't have, or a commute that makes it not worth the earnings. I need to find something soon. The money I put away when I was still with Dawson is slowly dwindling. It shouldn't be this hard to find something on the East side of Dallas.

"Did you hear me, Sophie?" Mom is by the counter, and I jump.

"You scared the crap out of me," I breathe. "And yes, I heard you."

"I called your name three times," she rolls her eyes. "You were staring into space. So, how's the search going?" She grabs an apple from the fruit bowl and takes a bite, waiting for my reply.

That makes twice she's asked me within the hour, and I get the message loud and clear. As much as my parents love me... They want me out. Not that I blame them. My little brother is getting ready to spend his last summer at home before heading off to fulfill his Ivy League dreams in another state. He may drive me nuts most of the time, but I'm proud of the kid. Maybe he'll let me tag along on his road trip. It will be a good way to avoid my parents worrying gaze for a while.

"It's going," I mutter. "I'm either under, or over, qualified. Why isn't anyone calling me back?" I wave my hands at my laptop to emphasize my continued frustration.

"Well, maybe you should actually go to some of the places," she says. "It might be easier if they could put a face to a name. At least," she shrugs. "that's what we used to do back in my day before we had the internet. There wasn't an option to fill out an application online." Oh great, she's going to go on another one of her long diatribes. "We had to go to the location, meet with a manager, and fill out the application by hand." She mimics writing as if I can't understand what she's saying.

"Yeah, yeah. I get it. You had to do everything the hard way." Groaning, I shut my laptop and lay my head on top of it. "But, I guess I can hit up some of these places tomorrow."

She walks over and pats me on the back. "You can't stay shut in the house out of fear. If you happen to see Dawson while you're out, you can always find someone to help you."

While her reassurances are helpful, she's working on the assumption that people are inherently good. Maybe she's forgotten I was dating someone we all thought was amazing, but turned out to be a monster. "I actually thought about seeing if Jay would let me go with him, and his friends, on their trip this summer."

"Nope," she leans back and pulls her hand from my back. "You are not running away from your problems. I won't allow it, and since you are under my roof for the time being... What I say goes."

Ugh, I hate when she uses the "mom" voice. What she's saying makes complete sense. Dawson has already taken so much from me... my self-worth, sense of security, and my job. If I let him claim any other parts of my life, I might as well go back to him. I'm not going to do that. My strength is greater than my fear. At least, I hope it is. "Fine," I huff. "I'll go look for a job tomorrow."

"Good." She doesn't say anything else, just turns and goes back to the living room. Mom has done her duty of nudging me in the direction she thinks is best. Maybe it is and maybe it isn't, but her and Dad are the only ones I can turn to right now.

Friends would come in handy right now. There were a few girls I was close with from high school, and we talked every day. They were the ones I could count on to catch me whenever I fell. That is until Dawson came into the picture and my world started to revolve around him. Pushing away those closest to me was the dumbest thing I've ever done. If I hadn't let him have so much control over me, my friends could have possibly helped me before things between us got so bad.

Enough of this. I'm not going to spend the rest of the day thinking about what could have, or should have, happened. Scooting my chair back, I stand up and debate taking my laptop to my room with me. I know I should be looking for more jobs right now, but I don't have the mental capacity to deal with it. There's a book by Kandi

Steiner, sitting on my tablet, and calling my name. If Mom stops bugging me, I may be able to finish it today. The book kept me up way past my normal bedtime last night because of how much I connected with the main character.

Mom is on the sofa, reading a magazine, when I cut through the living room on the way to my room. She doesn't say anything to me, and I'm grateful for it. I fully expected her to stop and lecture me some more about finding a job. Maybe she's giving me this one free pass after seeing how down I was in the kitchen a few moments ago.

My tablet is lying on my bed where I left it this morning. With any luck, it hasn't died yet. Plopping on the bed and adjusting my pillows until I'm comfortable, I pick up the tablet and press the power button. Score, it's still living. The battery is low, but not so low that I have to plug it in. Not right now anyway.

Revelry is already visible on the screen, waiting for me to devour it. To pull me in and live among these characters. To hopefully heal myself in the process. If there is anything that can propel me in the direction I should be going, it's the power of books. The one thing I didn't give up to Dawson.

The lack of interviews, and all my problems, will still be waiting for me later. Right now, I need this time for me to decompress and let go of my worries for a bit. The only way I can do that is through the characters in this book.

adrian

TODAY IS the day for our weekend getaway. It's so hard to get a weekend off from the tattoo shop, since those are our busiest days. Drunken people looking to add their dates name to their bodies, no matter how much we protest. And teens trying to come in with a fake license. It's always amusing on those nights because Charleigh has zero patience with those people. But Miranda has been acting different lately, and I wanted to surprise her with a beach trip all to ourselves. No clients or late nights getting in our way, just us and the frothy waves splashing against the shore.

Shuffling through the laundry basket at the foot of my bed, I pull out enough clothes to last the weekend. It's something I should have done before, but I've been at the shop past closing time the last few nights trying to get people out of the door as fast as possible. Honestly, I think that is what is causing the strain between us. At the same time, she knew what she was getting into when she started dating me, and when I proposed. Nothing has changed. Hell, it's actually helped since Charleigh has started tattooing as well. The workload is more evenly spread out.

All Miranda sees, though, is late nights and fear that I'll find someone else. Hopefully this weekend shows her that she's it for me. She's all I want, and there will never be anyone else for me. If there was any doubt on my end, I wouldn't have asked her to marry me.

The front door opening then closing catches my attention. "Miranda?" I call out. When she doesn't answer, I walk into the living room. She's staring out the window, her arms crossed over her chest. "I'm almost done packing then we can head out."

She doesn't respond, or even look in my direction. Silence is never a good thing with her, it's something I've learned over the two years we've been together. If she's quiet, she's upset about something. "Is everything okay?"

Still nothing. Glancing around the living room, I notice the lack of bags. Dread builds in the pit of my stomach. "Did you leave your suitcases in the car?"

"That's what I need to talk to you about," she says. Her voice is quiet, barely about a whisper. She's finally looking at me, though.

"Are you not coming with me? Did something happen?" It wouldn't be out of the realm of possibility. Her job at one of the top advertising firms in Dallas keeps her pretty busy. They've been known to ask her to work over the weekend for some of their bigger clients. But they usually give her more than a days' notice when that happens.

Miranda leans against the window frame, massaging her temples as if she's suddenly been struck with a headache. "Nothing happened, but I'm not going to the beach with you this weekend."

"Why not?" I stammer. "I have so many things planned for us. This is supposed to be our weekend to get away from our busy schedules." If I sound like a child pouting because I'm not getting my way, so be it. I've been looking forward to this weekend for over a month. Time alone, just the two of us, without any other worries. Not to mention it was hard as hell to get off work since weekends are the best nights for tattoos. And... I'm losing out on tips that could have gone toward our wedding.

I take a few steps toward her, willing her to see how much I want her to go with me. "Talk to me."

The second her eyes meet mine; I'm not going to like what she's going to say. There's no regret in them, only resignation. She sighs so loudly that I feel like I'm missing some important piece of information. "This, you and me," she waves her fingers between us. "Isn't working. We are two completely different people, and want different things."

"What do you mean?" There's no way she can mean what she's saying. Things were going great between us.

A little tense at times, but overall, I think we have a solid relationship.

"I want more from life. If things at work keep progressing, I'll be up for a promotion soon. There's no way I can achieve that while I'm with you. We've been together for two years, and you're still only a tattoo artist."

Everything else she said doesn't bug me. It's that last statement that makes my blood boil. "I was a tattooist when we started dating. I'm always going to be one. It's my passion, and something I'm damn good at. It's not like I'm hurting for money." I spread my arms out wide to indicate the apartment I live in. It's not some massive living space, but it's downtown and nicer than anything I've ever lived in.

"I didn't mean it like that," she retorts. "I just thought you'd move on to something different. You'd dabble in this for a while until you figured out what you really want to do with your life."

"This is what I want to do with my life. It's what I've always wanted to do. Ever since I first put pencil to paper," I yell. "Where is this really coming from? Your parents?" Then a thought hits me. One I don't want to begin entertaining, but it would make sense with all the late nights and the distance she's put between us. "Is there someone else?"

She winces, and I know I've gotten my answer. "No," she quickly replies. "I just don't think we're at the same place in our lives."

"Don't lie to me, Miranda." What seemed like a spacious apartment moments ago now feels like a tiny box, suffocating me. "I deserve the truth, at least."

"I'm not lying," she says, softly. "Not completely. I haven't physically cheated on you. But there's a guy at work who lines up with what my parents want for me, and fits in with the career I'm busting my ass to achieve."

"So that's it, then?" I'm pacing back and forth, unable to stand still. The urge to take out my anger, and frustration, on the wall is hard to ignore. "You're going to throw away what we have, all the love I have for you, for someone who looks good on paper?" Coming to a stop, I turn and look at her. "If you didn't want this, why did you say yes when I proposed?"

"I, I don't know," she whispers. "I thought things would be different."

It's not often that I'm rendered speechless, but now is one of those times. Not once in this entire conversation, has she said that she's sorry, or gotten upset. It's as if I'm a passing phase for her. A toy while she sows her oats, when I've loved her with every fiber of my soul. "You need to go."

"Can we at least be friends?" She asks on her way toward the door.

"Are you fucking kidding me right now, Miranda?" The audacity of those six words make me see red. "No, we can't be friends. In what universe would you think that's even a possibility?"

"I was just hoping…" She begins, but I don't let her finish.

"There's nothing to hope for," I say. "I don't even want to look at you. I'll drop your things off at your office. But, before you go, I want the key back. You no longer have a right to come here."

Silently, she takes the key to my apartment off her key ring, placing it on the table before she walks out of the door without a backward glance. She doesn't even care that she just ripped out my heart and put it through a grinder. What we had was real, or at least, I thought it was. Apparently, I'm just another lovesick moron that fell for the wrong girl.

To make matters worse, I'm screwed on this trip. Everything is already paid for, and now there's no reason for me to go. I'm sure Corey will be okay if I come into work. There are a few concerts going on in the area, and that means an influx of people coming into the shop. The only difficult part would be tattooing people who are getting ink for the special person in their lives. That's definitely not something I want to be around right now.

Grabbing my bag from the bed, I make the decision to go ahead with the trip. I don't need her with me to enjoy the beach. Instead of it being a weekend of passion and love, I'll be using it to forget the first girl I've allowed myself to love.

sophia

ROLLING OVER, my face hits something cold and hard. Ugh, what the hell is that? I lift my face up and see my tablet smeared with drool. At least I had the good sense to take my glasses off at some point in the night. Buying another pair is not something I want to do. Wiping off the remnants of my sleep, I fully intend to pick up where I left off in the book I'm reading. To my horror, it's dead. I guess today is going to be filled with adulting and all that jazz. If I would have known how stressful being an adult was going to be, I never would have signed up for it.

The sun shining through my window is bright, and I squint my eyes trying to dull the brightness. Since I'm up, I may as well get dressed and actually go out job hunting. Don't get me wrong, I'm grateful for everything my parents have done, but I need my space. I've been on my own since I was eighteen, and being stuck in their house at twenty-four isn't my idea of a great time. There is a tiny bit of fear that Dawson will be lurking around the corner. It's something I can't help feeling, and it will probably be around for a while. I have to overcome it, though. If I continue to let him have a hold on me, I'll never be able to move on with my life.

"Are you awake, Soph?" Mom knocks on my door.

"Yeah," I mumble, stretching my arms. "I'm about to jump in the shower."

"Okay," she pauses for a second. "Are you going anywhere today?"

Very subtle, Mom. It would have been better if you'd just come out and ask me instead of beating around the bush. "Yes, Mom," I grunt. Swinging my legs over the edge of the bed, I stand. Sleep is what I really want. Reading always manages to keep me up until an unreasonable hour. "I'm going to check with employers today about a job."

"That's good." The smile can be heard even if it can't be seen. The feeling is mutual. Anything to get out of this house.

"I'm gonna get ready, and I'll be out there in a bit." Pulling clothes from my closet, I hate everything I have. The "interview" clothes I have are outdated, and sort of blah. Definitely not a good look when I'm trying to impress people. It might just be time to go shopping, but I'm going to wait until Mom can go with me because I'm still not completely comfortable going out for long periods of time. I need a buffer in case I do run into Dawson.

"I'll make you something to eat," She says before walking away. Her footsteps are muffled by the carpet, but she's heavy footed, so I always know when she's around. Unless, of course, she intentionally quiets her steps, not wanting me to know she's there.

The shower is going to have to be a quick one. I woke up later than I had intended. The book pulled me in more than I wanted sleep. It's a reader problem I've had since I was a child. One that my mom wasn't a fan of when it would take her ages to wake me up for school in the mornings.

While the water warms up, I stare at myself in the mirror. Long gone is the girl I used to be. She was peppy and full of life. All that's left now is a shell. Oh, I can put on a pretty smile and fake it like the best of them. But, inside is ugly. Inside is where I'm constantly questioning myself, and my worth. All the confidence I once had has burned to ash, and I fear I'll never get that back.

Steam fills the room. Crap, I almost forgot that I had the water running. Lifting the lever for the shower to begin, I hurry in. Shampoo runs down my forehead and into my eye while I'm rushing to wash my hair. Ugh, I hope this isn't an indication of how the rest of the day is going to be. Rinsing my hair, and my eye, I bathe and get out. That may be the fastest shower I've ever taken, but I really need to be out of the house soon. If I show up too late in the day to inquire about a job, employers are likely to think work isn't my top priority.

Maybe tonight I'll set an alarm for when it's time to stop reading so I can do it all over again tomorrow. My skirt and top are snug. It's not surprising since I haven't worn it in years, but it's still depressing. My hair is thrown into a bun, and I apply a neutral eyeshadow to my eyes before swiping a bit of mascara on my lashes. I look like a librarian. While I wouldn't consider that a bad thing, I'm uncertain of how employers will react to it.

A plate of waffles sits on the kitchen table when I walk in. Mom is getting the syrup and butter out while I fill a cup with cold water. My hands are unsteady as I lift the cup to my mouth. It could be nerves, or fear, but I'll have to push both aside if I'm ever going to get past everything Dawson has put me through.

"Eat up, Sophia," Mom nudges me toward the chair. "You're going to need the energy to get through the day." When I don't sit down, she gently pushes me. "I know it's scary, but you can do this. He's not going to be out there waiting to pounce on you. And… if he is, all you have to do is call the cops. There's a reason we got a restraining order on him."

"Thanks, Mom." I pick up the fork and cut off a piece of the waffle. They're one of my favorite breakfast foods, but today they have no taste. I have to take a drink of water to force it down. "What are my chances of finding a job today?"

"Well, it's not like I can guarantee that," she laughs.

"But you'll never know unless you try. I have faith that you can find something."

After taking a few more bites, I stand. "Okay," I sigh. "I've got this, and I'm not giving up until I find a job." Maybe if I visualize finding a job, it will come true. Giving myself a mental push, I stride toward the front door, grabbing my bag and car keys on the way. "I'll be back later, Mom."

"Good luck, honey." Her words hit me just before I close the door.

Another rejection. I should have known the shampoo in my eye was a bad omen. I've visited almost every single job I sent an application to online. Each one gave me some asinine reason why I wasn't a good fit for their company. A small part of me thinks every conspiracy involves Dawson. If they already contacted my previous job, then that nailed the head in the employable coffin.

Not yet ready to go home in defeat, I park in one of my favorite parts of Dallas. There's always something going on, music to be heard, and food to be consumed. There's a burger place that I absolutely love and used to go to all the time. That was before Dawson. Now, it's going to be the one good thing that comes from this craptastic day. It's the pick me up I need.

Music filters through the room as I walk in. It feels like coming home. Ridiculous, I know, since it's just a restaurant. It's a restaurant I liked before, though. This is one of the small ways I'm reclaiming my old self. The road to that will be long, and hard, but I have no doubt that I will come out of it just fine. Or, at least, I hope I will. With everything so up in the air, it's hard to see past right now.

The secluded booth in the back is calling my name. Before I have a chance to sit down, one of the waitresses, Ginger, is standing beside me. "Long time, no see," she smirks.

"I guess I deserve that," I say. Ginger has worked here for as long as I can remember, and she's always been my favorite. She even gives me extra when I order dessert. I like to believe she thinks of me as one of her kids. All of hers are grown and have gone on to live their own lives. "How have you been?"

"Well," she puts her hands on her hips. "I'm not getting any younger, that's for sure." Ginger looks me up and down before throwing her arms around me. "Where have you been? I've seen your parents in here a few times, but you are never with them."

"Making bad life choices," I say, pulling back from her embrace. "Now, I'm trying to put myself back together. Any chance y'all are hiring?"

"I thought you had a job."

"I did," sighing, I lower myself to the seat. "But I lost it because of my aforementioned choices."

Ginger frowns before sitting down across from me. It's a good thing she's worked here for so long otherwise the owner wouldn't be happy. "I don't think we are, but I'll check." She reaches across the table and pats my hand. "Do you want to talk about anything?"

"Not really." Glancing around the restaurant, I notice nothing has changed. The vibe and energy is the same as it was when my parents brought me here as a kid. "How are Annie and Jordan?"

"Oh, they're just fine," Ginger grins. "Annie started dating someone and plans to bring him home to meet me this summer. And Jordan," she sighs. "He's finally growing out of his rebellious stage."

"Oh wow," I lean back. "I didn't realize he was giving you so many problems."

She laughs, "It was only a phase. He has one more year in college, then he'll be set loose on the world." She stands up abruptly. "I almost wish he would have gone to school closer."

"Why is that? Do you miss him when he's away at school?"

"I do, but I always hoped you two would hit it off."

"No offense, Ginger," I snort. "I don't think that would be a good idea. Besides, I'm swearing off guys for a good long while. They are too much trouble."

"You're wise in your young age," she grins. "Do you want your usual?"

"You still remember what I order?" It's been a couple of years since I've been in here, and she has to have had many customers within that time period.

"Of course I do." She walks backward a few steps. "You are my favorite, and best, customer."

Shaking my head, I laugh. Ginger is one of the reasons this will always be one of my favorite places to eat. Even in a city as big as this one, she manages to make you feel important. "Yes, I'll have my usual."

"I'll get the order put in and grab you a drink."

"Thanks, Ginger." As soon as she's gone, I open my purse, rummaging for my tablet. It's not in there, though. This morning was such a rush that I left it charging on my nightstand.

Pulling out my phone, I open the reading app and pick up right where I left off. A book nerd is always prepared. With any luck, I'll finish this book before I leave.

* * *

My plate has been cleared from the table by the time I finish my book and close out the app. Words cannot describe everything I feel after reaching the end.

"You must have really liked whatever you were looking at," Ginger calls out from behind the bar.

There are twice as many people filling the room, and that is my cue to head home. As much as I want to be the social butterfly I used to be, I don't have the energy to interact with others tonight. "It was," I call back.

Shoving my phone in my purse, I scoot out from the

booth. "How much do I owe you?" Ginger is filling a drink order as I walk toward the bar.

"Nothing," she smiles.

"Nope, you aren't paying for my meal, Ginger. I'm capable of buying my food."

"I know that, honey. Let me do this for you." When she sees my frown, she continues, "Consider it a good deed, and maybe it will bring more good things your way."

Arguing with her isn't going to do any good. Once she's decided on something, she doesn't change her mind. "Fine," I grumble.

"Oh, before I forget," she reaches under the bar. "I packed up a few slices of cheesecake for you, Jay, and your parents."

"You didn't have to do that."

"I know, but I wanted to." She places the bag in my hands. "Now, don't be a stranger. I shouldn't have to wait a couple of years before I see you again."

"Yes, ma'am," I turn toward the exit. "And thank you for dinner. I really appreciate it."

"Anytime, hon." She goes back to pouring drinks.

Before I walk out, I find another waitress, and pull a twenty out of my purse. "Can you make sure this gets added to Ginger's tips?"

"Sure thing," she nods and continues toward a table at the front.

The night air is hot and sticky. It's like walking into a sauna after being in frigid temperatures. The tattoo shop across the street catches my eye. There are a few people milling about, and I walk across the crosswalk.

After reading Steiner's book, I feel the need to ink something on myself as a daily reminder. My mom would freak out if she knew I was considering getting a tattoo, but something is pulling me toward this shop.

Grabbing my phone from my purse, I quickly take a picture of the name. I don't have time to see if they have any openings tonight. The cheesecake slices will get nasty if I keep them out in the heat for too long.

As soon as I'm in my car, I contemplate all the possibilities of ink. It would definitely be a change for the new me. Well, the new old me.

FOUR

adrian

THE PHONE RINGS. The device vibrating against my nightstand. It will go ignored once again. I don't have the energy to deal with her. She had my whole heart and treated it as if it didn't matter.

Miranda has been calling daily since I told her to get out. The same sob story that she loves me and she's *sorry*. Too bad "sorry" doesn't fix my faith in her. There isn't anything she can do to regain my trust, and I wish she would get that through her stubborn head. She can go on and live her perfect on paper life. I'll get over it...eventually.

All of her things are gathered in a single box next to the closet door. I haven't had the gumption to take it to her. Maybe that's why she's calling, to get her things. Her voice doesn't hold the emotion it should to want to make things work between us. But she didn't have much stuff here. That simple fact punches me in the gut. Most couples who have been together as long as we have would have more than what can fit into one box.

A small part of me wants to hear her out. To give into my screaming heart, and let her back in. Let her have all the pieces of me, even after her betrayal. The larger, smarter, part of me says to be done with her. Not to let her get inside my head again. No matter how much it hurts without her by my side.

Hell, I would be surprised if I was only a means to an end. Another sucker in the list of guys she has made fall in love with her, only to rip them to shreds in the end. It makes sense. Why else would she choose a guy like me? Someone who's so far beneath her social standing. Not that I think she's better than me. It was just odd that we struck up a conversation in the coffee shop that day. She pursued *me*. Maybe she came to love me in the time we were together, maybe not. But she didn't have to say yes when I asked her to marry me only to start "talking" to some other guy at her job.

Stewing over the bullshit with Miranda isn't going to solve anything. It's only going to piss me off more than it already has. Besides, I have a clientele that has proven to be more loyal than *she* has proven to be. Working at Life in Ink is my dream job, and not even Miranda can sway me to leave. I can't help but feel like that would have been her next step in our relationship considering what she said the day everything fell apart.

Oh well. There are appointments that are waiting on me, and it's time I get to them. Grabbing my wallet and phone off the nightstand, I walk toward the front of my apartment before pausing. A glance at the box of Miranda's crap pushes me to pick it up off the floor. Hanging on to this stuff will only make things more difficult for me. Make it harder for me to keep my focus off of what could have been instead of what I already have. Looks like there is one stop I need to make before I go into work.

The walk from the parking garage to the building where Miranda's office is located is brutal. It's the last time I'll ever step foot into this place. And, maybe the last time I'll ever see her. If all goes well, I won't even have to see her now. The box in my hands feels like deadweight, and I'm anxious to finally let it go. It hasn't been *that* long since I broke off my engagement with her, but it also feels like it happened ages ago.

It's funny how time flows. One moment can last a lifetime, and a series of events can pass in the blink of an eye. I don't know where my relationship with Miranda fell. Somewhere in between, I think. I'll move on from this, eventually. Right now, though... It still hurts.

The front of the building is solid glass, and I breathe a sigh of relief that she is nowhere in sight. That will make this a hell of a lot easier. A uniformed guard sits behind a counter when I walk in. I can't help wondering why this building needs a guard. It's something I never thought about before. Sure, there are other companies here, but I didn't know they were high profile enough to warrant the need for security. Oh well, after today it's not something I'll have to think about again.

"What can I help you with today," he asks before I've made it to the check-in desk. His eyes never leave the computer screen in front of him.

"I need this delivered to Miranda North," I answer while setting the box on top of the counter. It makes a loud thump, and the contents clang when I release my hands.

The guard's eyes finally pull away from the screen, and he eyes the box skeptically. "Is there a reason you don't want to take it up yourself?" He's staring at me like I may have put something harmful in it. Sorry sir, but I'm not that kind of guy.

"We broke up, and I'd rather not see her if I don't have to." Pushing the box toward him, I nod. "I can take everything out and show it's safe if you'd like."

The elevator dings just as the guard begins speaking, "That's not necessary."

He's saying something else, but I'm not listening because Miranda's tinkling laughter can be heard when the doors open. Shit. This is not how I imagined this going. I'd drop off the box and leave. Piece of cake. Her being down here throws a wrench in my plans.

"Thanks, man," I mumble, trying to turn so my back is toward her. If I can just hold tight until she's out of the building, I can make my escape.

"Adrian," her voice is just above a whisper. "Is that you?"

Damn it. I look down trying to figure out what could have given it away. Then I see the ink covering my arms. Of course, she would recognize them. The guard gives me an apologetic look before I turn around and face the girl that broke my heart. "Um, hey Miranda," I wave my hand awkwardly then shove it in my pocket. Why the fuck did I just wave to her?

"What are you doing here?" Her eyes are wide, and I can't tell if she's mad, or genuinely confused.

With the hand not in my pocket I scratch the back of my neck. "I was just dropping your things off," I nod toward the box.

"Oh," her whole face deflates. Did she think I came here for something else? After schooling her features into indifference, she gestures toward the guy standing beside her. "This is Clarence. And this is Adrian."

Snorting, I pull my hand up to cover my face trying to play it off as a cough. From the scowl on her face it isn't working. "Nice to meet you," I hold my hand out to him. This has to be the guy she was telling me lines up with her career better than I do. She never gave me a name, but the close proximity of their bodies tells me it's true.

He stares at my tattooed arm, then at my hand before nodding and saying, "You too."

"Well," I rock back on my heels. "I better go."

"Why don't you grab lunch with us?" Miranda asks with a flicker of hope in her eyes.

That's going to be a big nope from me. There isn't a universe where I'd willingly agree to go to lunch with my ex-fiancée and the person she's seeing now. "I'll pass," I mutter. "I have a client that will no doubt be waiting on me soon." It's a tiny lie. I do have a client this afternoon, but it's not for another two hours. I just don't want to be in this awkward hell for longer than necessary.

"Oh, okay," Miranda's shoulders slump. Her need to be on friendly terms with me makes no sense. Part of me hopes it's because she still feels something for me, and that maybe it was *real*. But I know better. She only wants to feel better about herself, and having me as her "friend" will do that. "I guess I'll see you around."

The glare Clarence sends her way is comical. As much as he is the poster boy for her career and family, he won't be around for long if she doesn't act accordingly. And seeing tattooed ex-fiancés isn't something he'll be okay with. Now, or in the future.

Shrugging, I head for the door. "Bye, Miranda."

The pain and confusion is still there, but the door on this chapter of my life is now closed.

* * *

The shop is quiet except for Charleigh banging around in her area. She's on cloud nine since she was promoted from apprentice to artist. She reminds me of myself when Corey gave me a chance. She's crazy talented for a someone so young, but she's grown up in this shop. She's been here for as long as I have. Hell, Charleigh is more dedicated than I was at her age. I would party it up any chance I got, while she would spend her spring, and summer, breaks in the shop doing whatever grunt work we'd throw at her.

My client just left. The job took less time than I imagined. They changed the original intricate anchor to one that was smaller and simpler. Walking across the shop, I lean against Charleigh's door. "How are things going with pretty boy?"

She groans, "I wish you'd stop calling him that. He's not horrible, you know."

"I never said he was," I argue. "It's just most of us don't go for someone like that."

"You did," she snaps back, and winces. "Sorry, that was a bitchy thing to say."

Deep breaths. Things may be over between Miranda and I, but it still hurts. "It's okay. I deserved it." Maybe he'll be different than Miranda. He could actually care about Charleigh for all I know. Being burned by someone exactly like him makes me wary, though. "It looks good in here," I nod toward the wall next to the mirrors, changing the subject. If I don't, Charleigh will feel the need to talk, and I don't want to. Not right now. Maybe not ever.

"Thanks," she beams. "It's the complete opposite of

the other rooms. But totally me."

"True." It is, too. She tries to put on this badass persona, but she's so damn bubbly and energetic. It's annoying sometimes. "I think your clients will love it."

Leaving her to her task, I go back to the main room. We really need someone to answer the phones and take care of all the paperwork since Charleigh isn't the main person doing it anymore. We all pitch in, and it works for the most part. But we all have our own way of doing things and it can get confusing at times.

The bell above the door dings, and a girl walks in. She looks young, maybe Charleigh's age. "Can I help you?"

She jumps, started at the sound of my voice. "I have an appointment with Charleigh."

"Sure, what's your name, I'll let her know you're here."

"Oh, yeah, sorry," she pushes back a lock of hair. "I'm Sophia."

I turn abruptly, until my back is to her. "Charleigh, Sophia is here!" I call before facing Sophia again. I study the meek girl that just walked in. She's pretty, and looks scared shitless with eyes wide as she studies the art on the walls.

Intrigue bubbles up, and I do my best to stomp that shit down. I cannot be entertaining thoughts of this girl. Miranda just ripped my heart into shreds, and this girl definitely doesn't fit the type of person I should be pursuing. Frowning at my interest in her,

Without waiting for a reply, I shove a form toward her. "We need you to fill these out."

"Sure." The corner of her mouth lifts slightly before she grabs the pen and starts writing.

As soon as she's done, I attach it to one of many clipboards we keep under the counter. "Charleigh will be here in a moment."

As soon as the words are out of my mouth, Charleigh is walking out of her room. Finally. This girl is making me feel things, and I don't want to. Glancing at my co-worker, I introduce the two. "Charleigh, this is Sophia, your appointment," I point at her as if Charleigh can't see the woman standing in front of us.

She holds out her hand to Sophia. "Hi Sophia, I'm Charleigh."

"I'm Sophia," she places her hand in Charleigh's. "But you obviously know that already."

Charleigh looks over at me. "Did you get Sophia to fill out the paperwork?"

"Yep, it's all right here." My gaze never leaves Sophia, and that terrifies me. "You're good to go."

"Thanks. Follow me back, Sophia," Charleigh walks toward her room with Sophia trailing behind her.

Instead of watching her go into the room with Charleigh, I stomp toward mine. That girl is all sugar and spice. But I want to know what is hidden beneath those layers. Damn it, I can't be thinking like that. My room is clean, but I rearrange everything until I hear her talking with Charleigh about what tattoo she wants. She'll be gone soon enough and I'll be able to get my head back on straight. There's no time for anything besides work. Even if it's a mousy girl with long dark hair, looking as if she's running from something.

sophia

THE GUY who just stomped away is intense. It's almost as if I offended him in some way. Does my naivete when it comes to tattoos show? I don't mean to act like a complete newb when it comes to ink, but Life in Ink is fascinating. This is the first time I've ever been in a tattoo shop, and I can't stop looking all around at the art that surrounds me. Some of them may have been drawn by Mr. Broody.

Maybe he's having a bad day, and doesn't know how to "people" well. Who knows, but I glance back as I follow Charleigh, and watching him walk away isn't entirely a bad thing. Those jeans hug his butt just right. Ugh, Soph, stop ogling the hot guy. There is no room for men in your life, especially when the last one pretty much destroyed you.

Once I'm inside Charleigh's workroom, I come to a complete stop. It's not at all like I expected. All the shops

I've seen on TV are filled with dark reds and black. This room is the *complete* opposite. Bright colors fill the room. I would go out on a limb and say her favorite color is some shade of pink.

"Did you expect something different?" she laughs, breaking me from my gawking.

I nod. "I figured it would be a bit more tortured artist."

She shrugs, "Eh, broody isn't really my thing." I get it. A job doesn't define your tastes. Neither does your passion. I only wish I could find mine.

Charleigh motions toward a chair placed in the middle of the room. "So, what are you wanting to do today?"

As soon as I sit down, I clasp my hands together. Rubbing my knuckles with my fingers. The nerves are creeping in, and images of infected tattoos plague my mind. This won't be like that, though. I checked out the reviews before I called to schedule an appointment. Life in Ink is a highly recommended shop. "There are two that I want, but I'm not sure how I want them done." My knee starts bouncing on its own volition. Wondering if she can tell how nervous I am, I place my hands around my knee to keep it still. "I was hoping you could help me with that."

She studies me as if I'm a science project. "Sophia, have you ever gotten a tattoo before?"

Damn it, she noticed. I bet she pegged me as soon as I

walked into the room. "No," I shake my head. "Is it that obvious?"

"A little," Charleigh laughs. "But it's all good. We've all been there before, I just had the luxury of growing up in this place so I knew what to expect."

"Will it hurt?" I feel like a total dumbass for even asking the question. Of course, it's going to hurt. It's a needle, going into my skin.

"That depends," she sighs. "For some it can, but it's more annoying than anything else." She looks me over once again, and I can't help but feel like she's not comfortable giving me a tattoo. "Do you still want to do this?"

Fear of pain flashes through me, and I don't respond right away. If it hurts, and I no longer want to finish it, the tattoo is going to look stupid. Being a burden to Charleigh is the last thing I want to do. With both of my feet planted on the floor, I almost decide to walk out of this room and never look back. I'm too troublesome for her since I don't even know what I want. Giving myself a mental slap, I sit up straight. Dawson treated me like I was a bother, and I'm not. This tattoo is for *me*, and I intend to take back every part of me. Including being apologetic to those around me for no reason. "Let's do this."

"That's what I like to hear." She grins at me like she knew I was going to make that choice all along.

Excitement is starting to replace the nerves as I tell her what I want. "The words for one are 'more than enough, I am not broken.'" I wait to see if she has anything to say, but she only sketches away in her notebook. "The second one is the word 'Always.'"

Charleigh continues drawing, and sketching out what she thinks the tattoos should look like. She takes my words and makes them a work of art with intricate vines weaving through the words of the first one, and splashes of watercolor behind and around the second one. It's more than anything I could have envisioned. "Do you like them?" She asks without looking up.

"Yes," I screech. It's not the most ladylike of responses, but she doesn't even flinch at my outburst.

"Awesome." She stands to get another set of papers from the counter. Placing the new paper under what she's drawn out, she begins tracing the design. "What made you decide on these specific tattoos?"

"Well," I pause for just a second to gather my thoughts. "The 'Always' is from Harry Potter, of course. I've loved that series since I was a child, and it helped me through some pretty crappy situations in school." Taking a deep breath, I continue, "The other is my little reminder to myself after reading a book called *Revelry*."

Charleigh nods along as I speak. "I've never heard of it. I'm guessing you had a connection to it?"

Grabbing a water bottle from my bag, I open it. "You could say that," I take a sip of water. "I had just come out of a pretty rough relationship. And I felt, I don't know, like I wasn't worth anything. I lost myself. But this book, it spoke to me. It made me realize that I am so much more."

"You might be my new favorite client," she squeals. "Most people come in here and get tattoos that hold no meaning to them. They just felt the urge. But you… you have put so much thought into this." Pulling the top paper, she was tracing, away she holds up the design.

Her phone pings with an alert, and she takes a quick moment to respond. She grins while typing out the message, and I wonder who she's talking to. It could be anyone, maybe a boyfriend. After putting her phone away in a drawer, she turns toward me. "You ready?" I give her a slight nod, and she continues. "You can still sit in that chair, but I'm going to need you to lean your arm across the table."

Swallowing down my nerves, I answer, "Okay."

"You're going to do great," she squeezes my hand in reassurance. "Just let me know if you need a break, and I'll stop."

"Sounds good," a small smile forms on my lips.

Charleigh pulls a pair of plastic gloves out of drawer next to her, and makes a face as she puts them on. She must not like the way they feel. She flips a switch, and her tattoo gun vibrates. The sound startles me, and I jump. "It's just the machine," she answers my nonverbal question.

"I'm okay. I wasn't expecting the noise is all."

She dips the end of the gun into a small pot of ink, and smiles at me. "Let's get started, then."

When she starts running it over my arm, I jerk in surprise. The sensation is different. Not good, or bad, just something else. I relax as I become accustomed to the feel of it. I can't believe I'm getting a tattoo. The location probably isn't the best place if I'm going job hunting, but I can always wear a cardigan or a bunch of bracelets to cover them up.

The sound of the machine buzzing is almost enough to put me to sleep. My eyes are closing when the noise stops. "We're done," Charleigh grins.

"Wow, already?" Time went by so quickly. That, or Charleigh is really good at what she does. It's definitely the latter. The ink now decorating my wrists looks amazing. And to think I almost chickened out.

"Yep," she begins cleaning the area and putting things away. "The tattoos were small. If we were talking a bigger piece, then it would have taken much longer." She wraps my wrists in plastic to keep them from getting dirty. "You did really well considering it was your first time."

"Thanks," I mutter. "What do I need to do once I can take these off?" Holding up my wrists, I indicate the plastic.

"Keep it clean and put a little bit of lotion on them if they start itching or feeling dry. Other than that," she shrugs, "they pretty much heal on their own."

Seems easy enough to me. At least getting ink isn't all that high maintenance. I am going to need to find a job, though. One that is okay with tattoos, and pays well because I already know I want to add more art to my body. It was a weird sort of therapy. Each time the needle would pierce into my skin, the negative energy I've been holding onto would evaporate. "How much do I owe you?"

I give her what she asked for, plus a decent sized tip. Charleigh was able to put me at ease and make me forget that I was getting stuck over and over again by a tiny needle. I'm not sure anyone else could do that. Especially not the broody guy. Hell, I'd be terrified to let him put ink on me. I'm sure he's a great artist, but at the same time I couldn't stand to have his intense gaze on me the whole time. There's no way I'd be able to sit still.

"If you have any problems, let me know," Charleigh says as I walk out into the lobby.

"Will do," I call. "And be expecting me to come back."

"I have a feeling you'll be back sooner than you realize." She doesn't mean for it to come out creepy, I don't think. It did, though. Just a little, almost like a promise.

I take my time walking to the front door, hoping to catch a glimpse of Mr. Broody. Why didn't I think to get his name from Charleigh? Not that I'm interested, nope not at all. A small voice in my head calls me a liar.

Out of the corner of my eye, I catch a glimpse of him walking into a room in the back. It's not the same one he walked toward earlier, and I want to know where he's going. To find some privacy to call a girlfriend maybe? My shoulders slump at the thought, even though I shouldn't care. He's not my type. The complete opposite actually.

But what do I know about my type? The last time I put trust in someone he treated me like complete shit. Shaking thoughts of Dawson, and Mr. Broody away, I continue out the door into the hot afternoon air. It's time to show Mom my new ink. She's going to lose her shit.

It's been over two weeks since I got my tattoos, and Mom is still pissed. I should win an award for correctly pegging mom's reactions. Her outbursts included, "why would you mar your beautiful skin like that" and "you're never going to find a job with those on display." Let's not forget the part where she asked me why I had to get them in a place where everyone could see them.

I'm not questioning her opinion, or perspective. However, I'm giving her money while I'm staying here and I paid for the tattoos with my own money. While I may be under their roof, I'm not mooching off of them by any means...yet. If one of the many jobs I've applied to doesn't call me back soon, I'm going to have to swallow my pride and take any one I can get. Even if it's something I don't want to do.

Job searches are displayed on my laptop screen when the phone rings. It's the house line, and not my phone, so I don't pay it any attention. Scrolling through listings in my area is becoming tedious. Most of them are the same jobs I've already applied for... it seems as if it's *me* they don't want. Their loss. If one of them would give me a chance, I know I could show them everything I'm capable of.

There's a knock at my door. "Sophia," my dad says. "There's someone on the phone for you."

That's weird. Anyone who wants to talk to me would have called my cell phone, and it never rang. Only one other person would call this line, and I don't see my dad letting *him* talk to me. Unless he got someone else to call for him.

Worry niggles at the back of my mind. Setting my laptop on my bed, I make my way to the door, opening it the slightest bit. As if Dawson might jump out at me from somewhere. "It's not Dawson is it?" I ask, needing to make sure.

Dad shakes his head. "Some girl named Charleigh?"

My mind comes up blank for a second, until who she is dawns on me. Why in the hell would she be calling?

"Okay, I'll be right there."

"No need," he holds up the cordless phone. "I figured you would be okay with talking to whomever this girl is."

"Thanks, Dad." He turns and walks back toward the living room. "Hello," I say into the receiver.

"Hi, Sophia," she sounds nervous. "This is Charleigh from Life in Ink. How's your ink holding up?"

"Pretty good," I smile looking down at my wrist. Sometimes I'll catch the outline from the corner of my eye and freak out before realizing what it is. It's odd sometimes seeing something there that hasn't been there before. "I didn't know you made house calls. How did you get my number?"

"It was on the paperwork you filled out when you got your tattoo." Still it's weird that she's calling me.

"Okay," I ask, leery. "Did you need something?"

"Actually, I'm glad you asked that." Her voice is more confident now. "I remember you saying you were looking for a job, and we *really* need a receptionist. Is there any chance you might be interested?"

Thinking back, I try to remember when I would have said that. It had to have been when she was trying make sure I stayed calm at some of the painful moments. Do I lie and tell her I found a job, or mention my interest? Minutes go by. "Sophia, are you there?"

She seems desperate. To be honest, right now, so am I. Before I have a chance to change my mind, I blurt out, "Yes. I'd be interested."

"Great," Charleigh sighs in relief. "Can you come by tomorrow so you can go over the details with my uncle? He's the one that owns the shop."

"Absolutely," I beam. "What time do you want me there?"

"Any time after lunch. Corey doesn't do as many tattoos as he used to so he should be free."

"Thank you for thinking of me." Inside I'm squealing like a little kid. Talk about perfect timing. "I'll be there around one."

"Sounds great. See you then." She doesn't say bye or anything, just hangs up.

Clutching the phone to my chest, I collapse onto my bed, almost landing on my computer. It's not every day a job falls into your lap. Not only am I excited to be working with Charleigh, but maybe I'll get to see more of Mr. Broody. This job is going to be a piece of cake. I mean, it's a tattoo shop. How hard can it be?"

adrian

THE SHOP HAS BEEN BUSIER than ever since Charleigh started tattooing. And, I have the pleasure of being tortured by the sight of Sophia on a daily basis. It's not a bad thing. It does make things more difficult for me and my growing interest in her.

She's been working at the shop for over a year, and while she makes things a lot easier for us, every day I have to remind myself why it's a bad idea to date a coworker. I've been intrigued by her since the day she got her first tattoo. Then, she was a scared, meek girl. But now... she seems stronger, as if she's finally found her footing in the world and nothing is holding her back anymore. Everything from her hair to the colorful ink adorning her arms has changed. What was once long, straight brown hair is now a short blonde bob. She's bolder, and I think Bianca has a lot to do with that.

"Hey Adrian," Sophia leans against the door jamb. "Is

there anything you're running low on? I'm going to make a supply order in hopes that it gets here before this weekend."

She doesn't really have to do those orders because it usually falls on our shoulders, but she's doing her best to make sure she adds value to the shop. I don't know why, there's no chance in hell Corey would ever fire her. She keeps the breakroom and the lobby cleaner than Charleigh ever did, and makes the entire atmosphere better. Nobody likes working in a messy shop. I'm pretty sure if it was up to Corey, and it definitely is, he would have her come in and run the shop while he would stay home with his wife. Not that that would ever happen. He loves tattooing way too much for that. He'd most likely have withdrawals and call up here nonstop to "check in," causing us to get behind while we answer his questions.

"No," I glance at my supply drawer. "I'm good. I ordered extra supplies the last time."

She smiles at me and nods her head. "Good deal. I only wanted to check because as usual Bianca waits until the last minute to let me know she's running out of ink." Sighing she turns around muttering, "That's the one thing you don't want to run out of. How can you tattoo people without ink?"

She's adorable when she works on a task. Doing her best to make sure everything is perfect. My eyes catch on the pack of transfer paper sitting on my table. It's unopened, but she doesn't know that. "Actually, Soph, I need some more transfer paper." Any excuse to talk to her. When she's paying attention, I do my best to be a dick. There's no good reason why. But if she doesn't express interest, then I don't have to worry about any future relationship. Backward ass thinking, I know.

Sophia is back at my door within a minute. "You literally just said you didn't need anything."

Stepping to the right to block her view of my table, I reply, "I know. But I thought I would double check, just in case."

She lifts an eyebrow, and tilts her head to the side. Damn it, she's knows I'm lying. The shrill ring of the shop phone begins, and she rolls her eyes. "If you say so. I'll add it to the order." Turning, she hurries to the front desk picking up the phone just before it stops ringing.

This girl, no woman, needs to get out of my head. She's consumed my thoughts for a long time. At first, they were welcome, a way for me to get over the bullshit with Miranda. Now, it's hard for me to come to work and see her every single day. She's within reach, but I forbid myself from grasping onto her. I've already been left once for greener pastures, and I'm not going to willingly let it happen again.

Pulling my appointment book out of the drawer, I scan the pages to see how the rest of my day is going to go. Soph has the main schedule up front, and everyone usually asks her what their day looks like. Not me, though. I keep my own to cut down on my interactions with her. It's the only way I could think of to keep me in my area and away from her.

I breathe a sigh of relief when I see there are only five appointments. Hopefully they'll end at the time they are supposed to otherwise I'll be here late. My plans tonight include going to a bar, drowning in my sorrows, and finding someone to erase all thoughts of Soph. It's not likely to happen. There's no way anyone can drive her from my thoughts. I've tried to no avail.

* * *

I knew my lack of appointments was too good to be true. The first appointment went fine, and we finished the small ladybugs on her foot long before her time would have been up. It was the second one that screwed up the rest of my day.

That's my one issue when it comes to this job. You quote somebody a price and approximation of how long it's going to take, and they come in adding to the original design. Don't get me wrong, I have no problem giving my clients exactly what they want. But when the changes almost completely override what we had discussed, it not only puts a kink in my workday, it also cuts into other people's time and they aren't out of here when they expect to be.

Even though it's a Wednesday night, music can be heard from the bars up and down the street. I'm supposed to be at one of those bars right now, instead I'm cleaning up my workstation and making sure the rest of the nighttime duties are taken care of. A cold beer in my hand would be so much better. Hell, I may go grab a drink after this anyway. It's not like the bars are closing any time soon.

Turning the corner to enter the break room, I run into Sophia. "Oh shit," she shrieks and rubs her nose.

"Sorry, I didn't realize you were still here." It's odd because I am usually the last one to leave if I'm working at night. The break room is typically one of the last things I check. Charleigh has a tendency to leave her snack wrappers all over the table. "Are you okay?"

"I think so?" She's still rubbing her face where she ran into my chest. "You should consider working out less. That," she points toward my chest, "is a dangerous weapon. Are you sure you aren't hiding bricks under your shirt?" Her cheeks redden immediately, and she takes a few steps back.

I smirk. Not because I hurt her with my apparent dangerous weapons, but because I caused a reaction in her. It shouldn't fill me with joy, and I mentally kick myself for the feeling. She is *off limits*. Too bad the thudding organ in my chest isn't on the same page as my brain. "Why are you still here? The girls left an hour ago."

She winces. Maybe my voice was a little harsher than I intended it to be. "I know that," her chin lifts a bit higher, shrugging off my tone. "You still had a client, though. I stay until all of the clients are gone. It's what Corey and I agreed on, and I take my job very seriously."

My eyes roll of their own accord. "I never implied

that you didn't." Glancing over her shoulder to the breakroom, I ask, "Is everything in there, cleaned up?"

"Yeah," she sighs. "Why is it so hard for Charleigh to throw her wrappers in the trash? I've met her parents, and I know they didn't let her get away with that crap at home. She doesn't even do it in her own apartment. I don't understand why she does it here?"

"Because," I snort, "she's seeing how long she can get away with it before you say something to her."

"Are you kidding me?"

"Nope." My head moves back and forth. "She used to try to pull that crap with me before she graduated high school. I told her I wasn't her father and she damn well better pick up after herself." I shrug. "There hasn't been a problem since. Until you came along."

"I'd expect that crap from Bianca. She can be scary sometimes. But I never would have thought Charleigh would do that." Shooting a quick glare at the breakroom door, she says, "I guess I'm going to have a talk with her."

"Have fun with that." The light in my workroom is still on, and I walk back to turn it off. "Are you ready to leave?"

"Yep." She quickly walks to the front counter, and pulls her purse out from the bottom drawer.

I hold the door open for her, and lock up as soon as she's through it. "Let me walk you to your car."

"I'm perfectly capable of getting to my vehicle," she snaps back.

She's not telling me something I don't know. At the

same time… I notice how she only leaves when she can walk out with Bianca and Charleigh. She's cautious, and I don't want her to lose that sense of security. Even if she's being obstinate. "I know that. It would make me feel better."

"Fine," she huffs. Our cars are parked on the other side of the building. Parking this close is almost unheard of, but Corey pays for our spots so we don't have far to go. "Well, I guess I'll see you tomorrow." Her keys are in her hand and she presses the fob to unlock the car. Her face is partially hidden behind her hair, but I can see the relief flash through them at not having to walk alone.

"Yeah, I'll see you tomorrow." She closes the door, reverses out of her spot, and then drives away.

I don't stop watching until her car is out of eyesight. Even though she's trying to put on a tough facade, I can see she's scared of *something*. I just wish I knew what it was. "Not my problem," I mutter to myself. Instead of getting in my car, I walk across the street to the bar. The need to drown out my thoughts is overwhelming.

sophia

HOLY SHIT. Adrian talked to me, and he was *nice*. Not that he's never been cordial. He is occasionally. But tonight, he took an interest in my safety.

Maybe it's time I take Randall's advice and ask him out. You know, instead of pining for him from afar. Hoping he will finally notice me. The longing glances, and finding reasons to talk to him, are clearly not getting me anywhere. I wasn't sure if he felt anything toward me until earlier this afternoon when I was getting the supply order ready. There was a full package of transfer paper sitting on the table behind him. He wouldn't need more for months. There's only one reason he would have asked me to order more... he wanted me to come back so he could talk to me.

Cars fly by while I exit the highway. There isn't usually this much traffic out at this time of night. It's only ten, but most people are tucked away into their beds, preparing for another work day. Wednesdays are the only days we close early since it's almost always slow, and I can't wait to curl up on my couch with a book.

Headlights flash in my rearview, startling me. Any other day it wouldn't bother me. Something is different about this one, though. It is making the same turns as I am. My stomach is in knots, and telling me something isn't right. I learned long ago to trust that feeling.

My apartment is only a few blocks from my parents' house, but I don't want to go there. Not when I have the feeling I'm being followed. My mind flashes to Dawson as I turn left on the street where my parents live, and the car turns moments after me. I haven't had any issues with him in almost a year. Maybe I'm panicking for nothing, and the person in that car lives in the same neighborhood. It isn't something I want to take a chance on, though.

The car that was behind me speeds past me when I turn into my parents' driveway, shocking me. They are all of a sudden in a hurry after being a decent distance behind me this whole time. It's disconcerting, and goosebumps rise on my arms. That is *not* normal.

Minutes pass by. I don't know if I should go inside and tell my parents, or if I should shake it off and go home. Someone taps on my window, and I jump. A small scream escaping my lips. Jay is smiling at me through the driver's window. "You scared the hell out of me, asshole."

"I'm not the one parked in the driveway staring off into space," he laughs. "Are you going to come in, or sit out here like some sort of creeper?"

Even though I know my brother is just playing around, the word creeper coming out of his mouth sends shivers down my spine. Still not ready to go home, I wave him back. "Yeah, I'll come inside for a bit." He takes another step back as I open my door. "Something just happened, and I need to talk to y'all about it."

Concern crosses over his face, but he doesn't say anything. As soon as I'm out of the car, he gently shuts the door behind me. Who would have thought that I would go from so excited about Adrian talking to me to terrified in a matter of twenty minutes?

The front door is wide open because my brother obviously still does not know how to shut the door behind him. I'm just stepping over the threshold when I turn back to make sure my brother is following. He's not, though. He standing in the middle of the sidewalk, eyes roving the street in both directions. He must've had the same thought I did. I don't know if that is comforting, or if it only worries me more. "Are you coming?"

"Yeah," he runs his fingers through his short brown hair. "I'll be there in just a second."

Instead of pestering him about whatever he is think-ing, like I want to, I walk inside and shut the door behind. Yes, I know that he said he would be right in but I wasn't raised in a barn. And knowing my luck, Mom will yell at me for leaving it open.

"Hi, Honey." She doesn't even give me a chance to turn around or put my bag down before her arms are wrapping around me. "I wasn't expecting to see you tonight."

The air smells like cilantro, ground meat, and onions. My mouth begins watering even though I had a late lunch. "Sorry, I wasn't really planning on coming over either." She pulls back, releasing me from her embrace. Her brows furrow, and she frowns. I will do anything to wipe that worried expression off her face. So, I change the subject. "You do realize that yesterday was Tuesday, right?"

"What the hell does that have to do with anything?" She puts her hands on her hips as if my question offends her.

"You made tacos," I wave my arm toward the kitchen. "And it's Wednesday."

She rolls her eyes just as the door swings open and hits me in the back. "Damn it, Jay."

"Sorry," he mutters. "In my defense, you shouldn't be standing right in front of the door."

He has a point, but I'm not going to tell him that. "It's not my fault. Mom came at me like she hasn't seen me over a year. It's been like three days."

"Well, excuse me for being happy that my daughter is unexpectedly visiting me." She throws her hands in the air, exasperated. "Let's go to the kitchen so you can eat some tacos." She pauses and studies me. "Unless you're too cool to eat tacos on a Wednesday, and only eat them on Tuesdays." I'm not too cool to eat tacos on Wednesday. If it were up to me, I would eat tacos every day. "And Jay, shut the door. You're letting all the cold air out," she calls as she rounds the corner into the kitchen.

Jay pushes me forward in order to close the door. "You have barely been here five minutes, and I'm already getting in trouble."

Smirking, I walk toward the kitchen. "Better get used to it, little brother. You may still be the baby in this family, but remember... you're only here until the end of summer break. She has to get on to you, or smother you, as much as she can before you go back to school."

He mutters something under his breath that sounds similar to "brat" before turning toward the living room. "I'm assuming you'll want Dad here for whatever you want to talk about."

And just like that, my momentary good mood comes to a screeching halt. Neither one of my parents are going to take my suspicions lightly. Hell, I'll be surprised if they don't demand that I move back in. "Yeah, he needs to be here for this too."

"I'll go get him." He continues to the living room in search of Dad. I, on the other hand, go straight to the kitchen. As much as this conversation is going to suck, tacos make everything better.

Mom already has a plate of tacos and a few slices of lime on the table. "So, what happened?"

"Why would something have happened?" I'm playing dumb. She knows it, too.

"Because you show up here, unexpectedly, and sit in the driveway for minutes. Is it Dawson again?" She pulls out the chair next to me and sits down.

"Maybe," I whisper. "Can we wait until Dad gets in here?"

"I'm here, Soph," his deep voice is loud in the small room. "What's going on?" He looks tired. If I had to guess, he fell asleep watching TV, and Jay had to wake him up.

"Someone may have been following me home tonight. I don't know for sure because they sped off when I pulled in the driveaway, but I have a gut feeling he's following me again."

"Why didn't you come straight inside when you got here?" Mom pounds her hand on the table. Nothing fires her up like Dawson interfering with my life.

"I was freaked out, Mom." What else did she expect me to do? "I'm pretty sure I was in shock."

"When did your restraining order expire?" Dad cuts in before Mom can say anything else.

"They expire?" Seriously? I thought once you got one it was a done deal, the person it was against couldn't mess with you ever again.

"Yes, they expire, dummy." Jay sits on the table despite Mom's angry scowl.

"Then I guess it's expired now," I sigh. "He must have been biding his time until he could come close to me again. Can I refile it?"

"Yes," Dad says. "We need to get that taken care of as

soon as possible in case he tries anything. Why didn't you read the whole thing Sophia?"

"I just assumed that since he stopped harassing me, I'd be fine." How was I supposed to know the stupid order expired? The months following my break up with Dawson are a blur. Living in a constant state of fear, and never wanting to leave the house. He did that to me. I *allowed* him to affect me that much.

"You can't assume anything with a person like Dawson, Honey," Mom grabs my hand. "He was unhinged when you were together, and he didn't get any better when you left."

"You should probably stay here for a while," Dad suggests. "At least until you can get a new restraining order against him."

Color me unsurprised. I knew that was coming, but I'm not going to let that asshole scare me out of staying in my own apartment. "No, Dad. I have a place of my own. I can't let y'all rescue me every time something happens."

"That's our job as parents, Soph." He leans back in the chair. "We protect our children when they are in danger. And... you *are* in danger when it comes to him. Whether you want to believe it or not."

"Will buying pepper spray make you feel any better about me staying at me own place?" It's a long shot, but worth it.

"Nope," Mom pops the "p" as she shakes her head. "But, if Jay stays with you, we'll consider it."

"Seriously?" Glancing at Jay, I await his outburst at the unfairness of it all. But it doesn't come.

"Sorry, Sis. I'm with Mom and Dad," he shrugs. "You get me, or you get your old bedroom."

Dad gives him an appreciative smile. "So, what will be?"

There's no way around this. I can see it in the stony expressions on their faces. Groaning, I lay my head on the table. "Fine, you can stay with me, Jay."

"Not the choice I would I have made, but it's one I can live with," Mom pats me on the back before standing up.

"Go grab your crap," I wave my hand in the air. "I'm tired and ready to go home."

After we've told our parents our goodbyes, we head to my apartment. It's a short drive, but I'm still pouting. This is not how I planned on my night turning out. The original plan was to head home, think over Adrian's actions with me today, and figure out how to approach him tomorrow.

I'll be lucky to make into work tomorrow without my brother tagging along. Maybe I should text Corey to see if I can take a personal day. Not that I want to. They are all perfectly capable of managing the shop without me, but I don't want to let them down. As we pull into my complex, I decide right then and there that I will not let him scare me away from my job.

Jay and I will go see about a restraining order in the morning, then I'll go to work. Business as usual.

adrian

THERE'S A SINKING feeling in the pit of my stomach. The beer I'm currently holding does nothing to squelch it. Sophia has been long gone for over an hour, but the nagging feeling that I shouldn't have let her leave doesn't go away.

It has nothing to do with selfish reasons, either. The chance to hang out with her, away from everyone else at the shop. Even though the thought alone terrifies me, it's still not a good idea. It's as if danger is creeping around the corner. Not for me, but for her. The car that pulled out right behind her doesn't help things. I'm not normally the paranoid type, but something felt off about it. Maybe I should call her and make sure she made it home safely.

Music from the band playing tonight makes it almost impossible to make a phone call, so I decide to text instead. I could go outside; except I'm not going to.

Honestly, a text message feels safer. There's less of a chance of rejection, or hearing her tell me to mind my own business.

Adrian: Did you make it home okay?

Sophia: How did you get my number?

Adrian: Um... You gave it to all of us when you starting working at the shop.

No response comes through, and I text her again.

Adrian: Do you not remember? I can delete it if you want.

Sophia: No, it's okay. It's just you are the only person who hasn't used my number. It shocked me.

Adrian: I'm not as needy as the rest of our co-workers. :)

The band begins tearing down their instruments, calling it a night, and music filters through the speakers as I watch three little dots show up on the screen. They've been there for a while. Is she writing a novel?

I laugh out loud, earning a few stares, when her message finally pops up.

Sophia: I've noticed.

. . .

All that time for two words. Do I make her as nervous as she makes me? This whole schoolboy crush is a new feeling for me. Well, maybe not new, but it's been a while. I'm pushing thirty, and the last time I felt this way... I got burned.

Adrian: So, did you make it home okay?

Sophia: Yeah. Ran into a slight problem, but I finally made it home. Do you check on our other co-workers like this?

Adrian: Nope. Just the pretty ones.

I hit send before I can delete. "Fuck," I groan, and bang my head on the bar. That was completely out of line. Having feelings for her doesn't mean, I can try to chase her like a lion chases a damn gazelle. Not to mention, I sound like a total douche. She'll never respond after that. I've fucked this up without meaning to. Plus, I opened the door wide open on something I meant to keep firmly shut. My head jerks up when my phone vibrates in my hand.

Sophia: You think I'm pretty?

What the hell? This feels like a trick question. I may be the one who brought it up, but I wasn't expecting that response. Is she asking because she has feelings for me, and this is her way of hinting at it? Or, is it because she is genuinely interested in what I think?

Adrian: I mean, yeah, sure.
    Sophia: You don't sound confident in your answer.

She has to be baiting me. It's what Miranda used to do when she needed an ego boost. That woman would get under my skin, and ask until I gave her a favorable response. Looking back, I can see what a disaster we were together. We never would have worked out because she would always keep trying to shape me into the man she thought I should be. Instead of letting me be myself.

Sophia: Did I scare you away?

I completely forgot I was in the middle of a conversation before my thoughts turned toward the train wreck my life could have become.

Adrian: Sorry. I got distracted. I do think you're really pretty, though.
    Sophia: Distracted by what? Are you with someone?

Adrian: Only if you count a bar full of people as someone.

Sophia: After the night I've had, I almost wish I was at a bar.

Adrian: Do you want to talk about it?

Sophia: Honestly, not really. It has been a weird night.

The bartender announces that it is last call. That is my cue to leave. Even in the middle of the week, drunken idiots still act like, well, drunken idiots. It's not something I ever like to be a part of. Rushing to the bar to get those last couple of beers that isn't that important to me. I've never understood that mentality, but to each their own.

Adrian: That sucks. I'm about to head home, so I will see you at work tomorrow.

Sophia: I may be coming in late, but I will see you tomorrow. Good night, Adrian.

Whatever happened to her tonight must be kind of important. She never comes in late, or takes the day off for that matter. I only hope it's nothing too bad.

The streets are thinning out now that most people have gone home. I'm almost to my car when something catches my attention. The car that pulled out after Sophia is parked a couple of rows down from mine. Or, at least, it looks like the same one. The ball of worry I had earlier flares up again. Something definitely doesn't feel right.

* * *

The shop is a ghost town when I walk in, except for one person. Corey is standing behind the desk in the lobby, and it's odd seeing him there. He's rarely come out of his workroom since hiring Sophia. "What are you doing out here?"

"Soph is coming in late," he grunts. "Someone has to take care of the desk."

Leaning against the desk, I laugh. "You realize that we were capable of taking care of our own clients before she came along, right?"

"True," he nods. "But we weren't as busy as we are now. Since Charleigh started tattooing, and doing all the marketing stuff, we're booked out for weeks at a time."

Shrugging, I look around the shop. There used to be days we would only have one or two people max. Now... we almost always have our workstations full with people trying to squeeze in between other appointments. "At least we're bringing in clientele. It probably would have happened sooner if you'd promoted her when she should have been."

"I was waiting until she wanted it bad enough." He flips through the appointment book, seeing what our workload is for the day. "I couldn't have her thinking the position was hers without working for it."

"She cussed you out almost daily." There's nothing Charleigh hated more than having to clean up after everyone. But it was her job as an apprentice. We've all been there, and had to deal with the bullshit. It didn't help that Bianca would give her hell. I was shocked when they became friends. Now they hang out all the time. I'm sure a lot of that has to do with them dating best friends.

At the thought of dating, my mind wanders to Sophia. The car from last night is still bugging me. Is that the reason she's late today? "Do you know what's going on with Sophia? Why she's coming in late?"

"Not my business."

"Surely you're curious," I argue. "She hasn't missed a day since she's started. She has a better work ethic than most of us."

"I worry about all of you Adrian," he replies. "But I try to stay out of your lives as much as I can, unless you come to me." He shrugs, "It keeps me out of any shop drama that may creep up."

"Is that why you let Charleigh and Bianca have their argument last summer?" Part of me always wondered why he didn't step in. At least it happened after the shop closed and not when we had clients. That would have been bad for business.

"Yep. I'm not going to fight your battles for you." He stretches his arms out wide. As if encompassing the entire building. "We're family here. Always will be. And families fight."

That's no lie. I haven't talked to my own family in years because of their lack of support. They didn't like my profession, and I didn't care for how they would talk down to me. In the end, they were toxic and I had to do what was best for me.

"Good point," I knock my fist against the desk. "I'm going to get my room set up."

"We've got a busy day ahead of us," he closes the appointment book. "Hopefully the girls show up on time."

"Doubtful," I flip the light switch on as I walk into my room. It's already clean, but I need to get the sketches out for my clients today. Prepared is always the best way to be. Otherwise, we have angry people to calm down.

Every few minutes I glance outside my door to see if Sophia has made it in yet. But she hasn't shown up. I fully intend on asking her what's going on when she gets here. I know I said I wouldn't bug her about it. And, maybe I won't. Maybe, I'll take the opportunity to ask her on a date. There's no point in fighting my attraction to her any longer. Even if it goes up in flames.

sophia

"WHAT DO you mean I can't file another restraining order?" It's taking everything in my power not to jump out of this chair and pound my fist on the desk. This is not the outcome I was hoping for when I walked into the police department this morning.

The officer behind the desk, Officer Daniels, shuffles papers, avoiding eye contact with me. "Well, your previous order expired three months ago. That means we will have to set another hearing date for this one." My mouth opens, ready to give my argument, but he holds his hand up to stop me. "Let me continue. I'm not saying that it won't be granted to you. It very likely could." This time he looks me square in the eyes. "What I'm saying is, you don't have any proof that he is following you again. And, the fact that you haven't had any issues with him for almost a year doesn't show an immediate threat."

"But..." This whole thing is absolutely ridiculous, and

I shouldn't have to go through this again. "There is a chance that I can get the order back in place?"

He nods and opens a file folder, ready to place all of my case files back inside. Part of me wants to let go of my fear that Dawson is following me again. The other part, however, wants to fight it tooth and nail because I will *not* let him have any sort of control over me again.

"I'd like to set a hearing date then," I cross my arms over my chest and wait for him to give me the forms to fill out.

"Okay," he sighs, and hands the papers over. "I'll get this put into the system today, and let you know when your hearing is."

Pen in hand I begin filling everything out. It's going to make me even later for work, but my safety is what's most important to me. And, if I can get this in place, my brother won't have to stay with me anymore. Not that he's a nuisance or anything. And we always gotten along except for a few squabbles here and there. It's just that after texting with Adrian last night, it would be nice not having my kid brother around. You know, just in case.

After all is said and done, Officer Daniels walks me to the front lobby. Never would I have thought I would be back in a police station again. But here I am, going through the same motions I had to before. I could be freaking out over nothing; however, I'd rather be safe than sorry. And, on the off chance that Adrian is interested in me, I don't want Dawson hanging over us like a black cloud. Crazy ex-boyfriends are not good for any sort of relationship.

The distance to the parking lot is short, and I slide into the passenger seat of my car. "So, how did it go, Sis?" Yep, my brother has deemed himself my own personal bodyguard. If I go somewhere, he goes. It's the only way he thinks he can make sure I'm safe.

"Not great," I shrug. "Since he hasn't shown any harmful actions, and I don't know for a fact that he was following me last night, a judge most likely won't approve it. But there's a chance one might. I went ahead and filled out all the crap, and now I wait to see about a hearing date."

"Damn," he shakes his head. "That sucks." Putting the car in reverse he looks both ways. "Where to now?"

"Work." He stares at me like I've lost my mind. "Can we at least eat first? I'm starving."

"You can do whatever you want after you drop me off?" Seriously, it's not like he has to wait around at the shop for me to get off work. If anything, he should offer to bring me something. Does that cross his mind? Of course, not. "The burger place Mom and Dad used to take us is literally right across the street. I'm sure Ginger would be happy to see you."

He snorts as he pulls onto the road. "I'm sure she just wants to hit on me."

My hand flies across the space between us, smacking him in the chest. "Don't be so full of yourself. She only likes to give you a hard time. She knows it embarrasses you."

"Well," he huffs. "I wish she wouldn't. It's weird."

"You won't be saying that when an older lady catches your eye," I mutter.

"What was that?" He turns the radio down for me to repeat myself.

Giggling, I shake my head. "Nothing. Just drop me off and go feed yourself."

The tattoo shop is full of people when I walk through the front door. I didn't think today's schedule was quite this busy when I checked yesterday. I guess I was wrong, and I feel horrible for having to come in late. Corey is standing in my usual spot behind the front desk. He looks frazzled, and like he doesn't know what he's doing. Which is insane because he ran the shop just fine before he hired me.

He looks up to see who just walked through the door, and his shoulders sag in relief when he realizes that it's me. "How are you holding up without me, Boss Man?"

"Thank God you're back." He's already taking steps away from the desk as I make my way toward him. "It's been a madhouse. People coming in without appointments and I have no idea what your system is. I'm not even supposed to be here today." He throws his arms in the air.

This man is acting as if he's incapable of taking care of scheduling a few appointments, and I can't help but laugh at the whole situation. "It's only been a few hours. How did you manage anything before me?"

"For starters, all the artists handled their own appointments." He holds up the pointer finger on his right hand, counting off how things were done. "Secondly, we were hell of a lot less busy than we have been for the past year. And thirdly," he takes a deep breath. "You have spoiled all of us with your organizational skills."

I throw my head back in laughter this time. "It's nice to know you can no longer run the shop without me. Does this mean I get a raise?" This small interaction, no matter how trivial it is brightens my mood after being at the police station this morning.

"You're here now, and that means I can take the wife to the movies." He points at the stack of papers on the desk. "Have fun sorting the mess I left you. I didn't know what you do with everything. We'll talk about a raise in a couple of days. You definitely deserve one."

Waving him off I begin going through the papers. "Go have fun with your wife, I can manage from here."

He doesn't make me say it twice. He's out the back door before anyone else realizes he's gone. We don't want any disgruntled clients and I need to get some sort of order happening before that happens. Clapping my hands a few times to get everyone's attention, I stand on my tiptoes, and raise my voice, "If you already have an appointment, please have a seat on the right. I'll come by in a few minutes to get your paperwork all sorted out." The crowd parts like the Red Sea as they do as instructed. "The rest of you, if you could please form a line, we'll get your appointments scheduled."

As those still standing form a line, I begin passing forms out to the first group. It's not so hard when you place a little bit of order amidst the chaos. The papers Corey left on the desk can wait until later. Taking care of everyone that's here right now is more important.

"How much time do I have before my next appointment?" Adrian's voice comes from directly behind me.

I jump, and the papers that were in my hand now litter the floor. "Don't sneak up on me like that. I could have had a heart attack." I know that's not accurate, but I'm not a fan of being surprised either. It was one of the things Dawson used to do when he was upset with me for whatever reason.

"Sorry," he shrinks back. "I'll try to be louder next time." Leaning against the counter, he studies me. No doubt trying to figure out what has me so jumpy. "I'm going to order pizza for everyone since we haven't had much of a break. Are there any particular toppings you like?"

Who is this guy, and what did he do with the broody

Adrian I've known for over a year? He's never once ordered pizza for everyone as long as I've been here. Much less asking what kind of pizza I like. "What does everyone else want?"

"I know what they like," he smirks. "I'm asking what *you* want."

Not going to lie, I've always hated ordering pizza when it's not just for myself. Everyone tends to give me weird looks when I place my order. "Um, ham and pineapple?" Dammit. My goal wasn't to sound so unsure of my choice. It's my favorite, and I shouldn't be ashamed of it.

His nose scrunches up in disgust. "Seriously, that's what you like?"

And that's the look I always get. It makes me feel like I'm abnormal even though there is absolutely nothing wrong with fruit on pizza. "I'm okay with whatever everyone else wants," I relent. Trying so hard not to be the odd one out.

Adrian does his best to school his features, but I can still see that he thinks it's the nastiest combination in existence. "No, that's what you like and that's what you're going to get." Straightening up he grabs his phone out of his pocket. "I'm going to go order it. Can you let me know when it gets here? I'm sure I'll be in the middle of another tattoo by the time it arrives."

"Sure thing," I smile. Him ordering pizza is really weird. And him asking me specifically what I want is even weirder. I'm not complaining though. It means I don't have to wait until after midnight to eat. That happens way too often thanks to working in a place that stays open so late. Sometimes I miss eating at normal hours, but I love working at Life in Ink more. Sighing, I get back to work.

People are still coming into the shop. Some of them with appointments. Others wanting to book a slot with one of our artists. And a lot of them only come in to admire the artwork on the wall. I was shocked, when I first started working here, to learn that most of it was drawn by Charleigh. It's no wonder she's almost always booked solid. She has mad skills when it comes to design and creativity.

A delivery guy carrying a pizza walks inside and straight to my desk. "I have an order for Sophia."

"I think you mean Adrian. I didn't order anything." That's an odd mistake to make.

His eyebrows rise in confusion as he studies the order sitting on top of the pizza box. Maybe he has the wrong address because there is no way that is going to feed everyone in the shop. Or, the rest of the pizzas are in his car? I've seen the damage Charleigh and Bianca can do when it comes to food. We would need a minimum of four if I wanted any.

"It looks like it was ordered, and paid for, by Adrian. But the instructions say to give it to you." He holds out the paper as if I would question him.

That sounds about right since he mentioned he would be with the client by the time it was delivered.

"Okay," I bend down and grab a few one dollar bills out of my purse. "I will make sure he gets it." He hands over the pizza without another word and I set the tip money in his hands.

As soon as the delivery driver is out the front door, I lift the top of the pizza box and take a peek. The whole thing is a ham and pineapple pizza. Not what I was expecting after the look of horror he gave me. Instead of letting the girls know there is food, since he seemed to have ulterior motives, I march straight to his room.

There's a girl lying face down on the table with her shirt off. I've worked here long enough that this shouldn't cause me to blush, but it does. Chaleigh has done all of my tattoos, and I'm not sure I could undress for one with a guy I barely know. Twenty-One Pilots is playing through the small speaker he keeps by the door. I watch him work for a few minutes, admiring his work, and not wanting to spook him. It wouldn't be good if he jacked up her tattoo because of me.

Finally, he lifts his hand from her skin, and I clear my throat. "Want to explain why there is only one pizza?"

His cheeks redden, and it makes him look boyish. This toned, completely inked, and focused guy I've been admiring for months is blushing. Inside I'm melting into a puddle of goo, but on the outside... I only lift an eyebrow waiting for a response. It's a tactic my mom uses when she's being serious. Hopefully it will work on him, too.

He opens his mouth then closes it. After shaking his

head, he responds, "I didn't see that sparkly lunchbox you usually bring in the breakroom. I figured you might be hungry."

"Oh," I jerk my head back. "Thank you." Glancing back into the lobby, I make sure nobody needs me. "But I thought you were getting food for everyone."

"Well," he laughs. "I didn't think you'd let me buy you dinner if I told you I wanted to."

He has a point. It's not that I'd feel like a charity case if he did, because let's face it. The past twenty-four hours have been anything but normal. Adrian has been the main thing that's had my mind suffering whiplash. After pining for him for a long time, he's finally showing interest. I can't help thinking that maybe he wants something from me, or he's just screwing with my head. It's not an unlikely possibility after the disaster my life became with Dawson.

"Seriously, thank you," I say while backing out of the room. I wasn't hungry before, but now that I'm not busy... My stomach is demanding food. "I can save you a few slices if you want me to."

"No thanks," he glares at the pizza box. "You couldn't pay me to eat that."

"You don't know what you're missing." I turn around, wanting to grab a plate out of the breakroom so I don't make a mess at my desk.

"What are you doing after work tonight?" He asks, and I stop in my tracks.

"My brother is picking me up and taking me home." I

don't want to mention that my brother is also sleeping on my couch to protect me from the craziness that may be following me once again.

"Go out for a drink with me." He's not asking. At the same time, he's not really demanding it either. His voice is raised ever so slightly, hoping I'll agree.

"I don't know," I hedge. As badly as I've dreamed of this moment, I'm not sure it's a great idea right now.

The girl he's tattooing lifts up just a bit, enough that she can see me without exposing herself. She nods her head and mouths, "do it," with a wide grin. Why is this girl I don't even know invested in me saying yes?

"Come on, Soph," Adrian argues his point. "What are you going to do when you get home? Watch some TV then go to bed? Having a drink with me won't put much of a delay into that, and I'll drive you home."

Biting my lip, I weigh the options in my head. Go home and hang out with my brother. Or... go have drinks with the man I've wanted so desperately to *see* me. I'd be insane not to take him up on his offer. "Okay."

He smiles so big you can see the happiness in his eyes. "We'll go across the street. They probably have a band coming in tonight."

Without saying another word, I take my pizza directly to my desk. Screw the plate. I'll eat straight from the box. Besides, that's where my phone is, and I need to text my brother.

. . .

Sophia: Don't worry about picking me up.

Jay: Why?

Sophia: Because I have a date. I think?

Jay: Be careful. Keep aware of your surroundings, and call me if you need rescuing.

Sophia: Yes, sir.

Jay: I'll be here when you get home.

I can't believe this is happening. Screaming from a mountain top couldn't make me any more excited than I am right now. Too bad Jay will be in my apartment when the night is over.

adrian

I CAN'T BELIEVE I just asked her to have a drink with me, or that she even agreed. Raven, the woman lying on my table, told me I should ask. Some people pay therapists hundreds, or even thousands, of dollars to spill their guts to a person sitting behind a desk. I'm not knocking therapy. It's always a good idea to keep your mental health intact. But Raven is someone I've been working with for years. She probably knows me better than anyone.

"What did I tell you?" She laughs. "All you have to do is ask." I want to argue with her. Tell her all of my doubts and reservations. But she continues, "Don't bother telling me what a bad idea this is. You need to live your life, and *stop* living in fear of someone screwing you over the way Miranda did."

"I wasn't going to say that," I mutter. It's close to

what I was going to say, but she doesn't need to know that.

"Yes, you were," she accuses. "Anyway, you need to finish up my ink or you won't be able to get drinks with your crush."

"She's not a crush." Dipping the needle into the ink pot, I continue working on the flowers going up and down the side of her back. We've been working on it for a while. She'll have one on each side by the time we're done. Raven will be in here in another two weeks to continue working on it.

"You know you don't have to lie to me," she says into the silence, scaring the hell out of me. I thought she had zoned out again. "You've been talking about her for months. If that isn't a crush, I don't know what is."

"It's complicated," I sigh. "I like her... *a lot*. There are days she seems like a complete badass, and others when she's as fragile as porcelain." Today is one of the fragile days. Sophia tries her best to hide it, but something is hurting her, and as much as I've been fighting it, I want to be the one she confides in. Even though she's friends with Bianca and Charleigh, I don't think they know the full extent of who she is. We all get the tip of the iceberg, and I want to know what's below the surface.

"Okay, Romeo," she mutters. "Let's get this section done. It looks like we both have dates tonight."

"You didn't tell me you had a date." If she had, I wouldn't have spent so much time talking to Sophia just now.

"What are you? My father?" She shakes her head the slightest bit, doing her best not to move the rest of her body. "I don't tell you about all the guys I date. I'm just having fun right now until there is something to tell you about."

"You're being careful right?" Raven is like a sister to me at this point. Seeing her every couple of weeks for new ink is bound to form that bond.

"Yes, Adrian." Even though I can't see her face, I'm ninety percent sure she just rolled her eyes at me. "I'm being careful. Geez, it's not like I sleep with every guy I go on a date with."

"Good," I nod. "You never know about people anymore. There are a lot of weirdos out there."

"I should know. I'm one of them." She looks over her shoulder to see the progress. "Now, less talking, more tattooing."

Who am I to argue with her? She's right, there's only a bit more of this design that I have to finish, and she can go meet whoever this guy is. And I can go out with Sophia. Hopefully the nerves taking up residence in my stomach don't make my hands shake too much.

* * *

The shop is *finally* blessedly quiet. Everyone is cleaning up their areas, ready to put this busy day behind them. I'm not sure what they are complaining about. It's only

Thursday. We still have two more long days ahead of us before we get an easy one.

Sophia is talking to Charleigh and Bianca when I walk out of my room. "Ready to do this again tomorrow?"

Charleigh groans and drops her face into her hands. "Can I call in sick tomorrow?" Her voice is muffled but we all know what she's saying.

"Nope," Sophia shakes her head. "I'm not going to be the one responsible for calling all of your clients. You're booked solid through Sunday."

"That's it," Charleigh throws her arms in the air. "I'm going to go hang out with Layla at her daycare. Maybe one of them will get me sick."

"Don't even think about it," I warn. "People were not happy when you ran out in the middle of the day last summer. Your customer base has only gotten bigger, and you don't want that many people pissed with you."

"Fine," she pouts. "I guess I'll just go home and get some sleep."

Bianca is doing her best not to laugh. She was always crazy busy before Charleigh started tattooing, but I think she likes the free time she has now. "That sounds like a better plan. I don't have to be taking on your angry people."

"Okay, okay," Charleigh holds her hands up in surrender. "I'll be here. Who knows? Maybe I'll even come in early."

"Don't get our hopes up," Sophia says while grabbing her purse from under the desk.

"Do you need a ride home?" Bianca is digging her key out of her back pocket. "I noticed your car wasn't outside when I grabbed food earlier."

Sophia sneaks a sly glance in my direction and she blushes. "No, I've got a ride home."

"All right," Bianca says, eyeing both of us suspiciously. "See everyone tomorrow."

Bianca and Charleigh walk out of the shop together, talking about some book club they are a part of. I didn't realize either one of them read outside of tattoo magazines. It's an asshole thing to think, but I've only ever seen them with magazines about tattooing. The shop is completely silent. If I listen close enough, I'm almost certain I can hear my own heartbeat. It's rapid thump, thump against my chest is a little annoying. Not even Miranda made my heart race like this in the two years I was with her. Proposing to her was definitely a mistake. Especially if I didn't react like this to a girl I supposedly loved, but I am to a girl I'm *only* interested in.

Sophia is playing with the ends of her short hair, looking everywhere except at me. It's cute that I make her nervous. Miranda was a force to be reckoned with, demanding everyone's attention. The woman standing before me doesn't always want that sort of thing, but she's strong in her own ways. How many other people can get a shop full of tattoo artists to get their act together like she did?

Breaking the awkward silence, I take a small step toward her. "Are you ready to go?"

"Oh," she shakes her head. "Um, yeah. Where are we going?" She glances around as if waiting for someone else to answer even though she knows we're the only two left in the shop.

"It's not far." My hand itches to grab hers. I don't, though. This is just a drink, not a date. Besides, I don't know what her boundaries are when it comes to hand holding. Maybe it's not something she likes. Instead, I nod my head toward the door, "Come on," and she follows me as I open it.

With the shop locked up, I start walking toward the crosswalk, Sophia close behind me. The streets aren't as packed as they will be tomorrow night with people on their way to concerts and clubs. This area is usually pretty busy, but it almost doubles during the summer. It's a unique part of town with shops of every kind lining the street. I couldn't imagine a better place to work, or live.

I open the door to the restaurant and bar that sits directly across from Life in Ink. I know she's gotten food from here before, we all have, and I want her to feel comfortable. That's what is most important to me right now. That she trusts me, and sees me more than the asshole vibe that I give off at work. That's not me, not really. It's what I do to keep everyone else at bay.

"We're going here?" She smiles as we walk inside. "I love this place."

"I did good, then?" My heart skips a beat at the joy coming off of her right now.

"Absolutely." She grabs my hand and leads me past the bar to a booth in the back. It's a good thing, too because all the seats at the bar are taken. Most of the booths are, too with only a few tables sprinkled throughout the room open.

God, I hope she doesn't notice how sweaty my palms are. My body, and nerves, need to get their shit together. I'm not a fifteen-year old boy anymore. I'm a grown ass man that shouldn't be freaking out over the touch of someone else. It's never happened before. Not with Miranda, or the girls I've seen in between. None of them had the potential for anything more. With Sophia, I can almost see some sort of future.

Before we're completely seated, Ginger, one of the waitresses is already at our table. "Funny seeing you two here... *together*." She winks at us, and Sophia's cheeks turn a bright red. "What can I get you started off with, Sophie?"

Sophia doesn't bother looking at the menu. "Cheese sticks and whatever hard apple cider you have tonight."

"And you, Adrian?" One of my favorite things about this place, and the staff, is that they know who we are. I mean, they should since we're in here all the time. It's the closest place to the shop and we know we'll get good food to tide us over through our long work nights. And, they're still open after we close up for the night. It's a win all the way around.

"How about a *Coors Light* and an order of cheese fries."

"Do you want them loaded," Ginger asks.

I glance at Sophia and she shrugs. "Sure. Thanks Ginger."

"Anytime, Hon." She backs away. "I'll be right back with your drinks."

Sophia getting her purse situated next to her. No doubt doing anything to avoid eye contact. "Did she just call you Sophie?" Worry that I've been saying her name wrong this entire time gnaws at my gut.

"Yep," she nods. "She's done it since I was younger. Sometimes she calls me 'Sophia,' but it's almost like adding that extra letter is too much effort sometimes." She studies the walls, although she's most likely seen them many times if she's come here as long as she says she has. "I'll answer to it though. Jake, Marshall, and Randall all call me the same thing, despite Charleigh always correcting them. It doesn't bother me."

That's good to know. But I love the way her name rolls off my tongue, and I doubt I'll ever be able to call her Sophie. It's too cutesy. And while she is very cute, in my opinion, she's so much more.

"So, you've been coming here a while?" I have to raise my voice over the band playing. Maybe it would have been smarter to take her somewhere a bit quieter. A place where I could really get to know her without competing with the band and background noise.

"Yep." She's looking at me now, and I wonder what

she sees. "My parents found this place on one of their date nights, and thought Jay and I would love the food. They never brought us here at night," she swings her arm out, indicating the vibe in here. "But we would come on Saturday, or Sunday, afternoons."

"So, Ginger has pretty much seen you grow up?"

Speak of the devil. She slides our drinks onto the table. "Here you go. They are working on your order right now. Call me if you need anything." And just like that she's gone again. Off to take someone else's order or refill their drink.

"Yeah. She's the one I would go to when I was having boy problems in school." When I raise an eyebrow in confusion, she adds, "She is like a mom figure without actually being my mom. It helped sometimes."

Grinning, I tap my chin. "I'll have to ask her all about your awkward phases as a kid. And for direction on what I need to do to keep you from going to her about me."

Groaning, she hides her face in her hands, but looks back up at me seconds later. "Please don't. That would be beyond embarrassing. There's no telling what information she would give you."

"All the more reason for me to talk to her," I take a drink from my beer, and cold liquid soothes away some of my nerves. "You know if you tell me not to, I'm more likely to do it, right?"

She rolls her eyes. "Then by all means, go get whatever juicy information you think you need."

Well damn. She just took all the fun out of it. I'm only

teasing her, though. Getting a shortcut to who she is would be like cheating to get to the prize. I want to learn everything about her from her by talking with her and doing things with her. It's the one thing I hate about dating in today's world. Everything is online and through moments people want to show you. Gone are the days when people actually went out and talked instead of staring at their phones the entire time. Fuck, I sound like an old man.

The band on the corner stage has gone silent, getting ready to play again or take down their equipment, I don't know. My attention has been on the woman sitting across from me. Sophia uses it to her advantage. "How long have you been tattooing?"

"Six or seven years," I shrug. "It's hard to keep count sometimes. I love this job, and most days it doesn't feel like one, you know. How many people can honestly say they are excited about going into the office?"

"Not many," she agrees. "I liked my last job well enough. But I really like working at the shop. Every day is something new, and I get to meet so many different people."

Ginger slides our food, and a couple of plates onto the table without interrupting us. But the huge smile she wears on her face can no doubt be seen by everyone. Aside from Raven, she probably knows about the heartbreak Miranda dealt me. I came in here often enough after the breakup to soothe my aching heart with beer after beer.

"Exactly. It's always a new adventure, and you can see into a person based on the ink they want." I point toward my huge plate of cheese fries. "Want to share?"

"Sounds good to me. I always forget how big their appetizers are." She looks around conspiratorially. "Either my eyes are bigger than my stomach, or Ginger finds a way to add more food to the portion."

Chuckling I shake my head. "It's probably a combination of both."

"Most likely," she shrugs. "She does always give me extra dessert when I come in."

"That's not fair," I gasp in mock surprise. "I want extra dessert. I'm going to have to say something about it."

"And then you'll get no dessert," Sophia sing songs. "Ginger can be evil that way. One-time Jay, my brother, was being an ass and when she brought out our slices of pie, she gave him a crumb." She laughs loudly at the memory. "He totally deserved it, and he stopped acting that way when we would come eat here."

"Did she end up giving him the rest of his pie?"

"Yeah," Sophia sighs. "You know Ginger couldn't hold out on him for long. But she did make him wait until I was halfway finished with mine. She's the best."

Ginger really is, and she has a great sense of character judgement. If she thinks highly of Sophia, then I may be safe in possibly dating her.

sophia

ALL THE FEARS and doubts about having drinks with Adrian were completely unnecessary. Tonight, has been fun. It's been way too long since I've allowed myself to go out and enjoy the company of another man. Anger at allowing Dawson to still have that sort of sway over me rises up, but I push it down as far as I can. *He* will not be allowed to taint this night.

Adrian and I have been talking about nothing and everything. Tattoos, life, my family. He asks me questions nobody has ever thought to ask, and they are about *me* rather than just filling space so he can't talk about himself again. It's crazy how we've worked together for so long yet we know absolutely nothing about each other.

"Why was your brother going to pick you up tonight? Is something wrong with your car?" His brows are furrowed in concern. "I know a guy that can have it working in no time."

A part of me wants to lie. Wants to tell him that something messed up on it, and that is why my brother has now become my chauffeur. But I can't do that. Lying is the one thing guaranteed to push him away, and I've already started springing up thoughts of date nights, holding hands, and snuggling during movies. This is why it was a bad idea to have drinks with him. The first sign of attention and I'm conjuring happy ever afters.

"No," I shake my head, and look down at the bowl of marinara sauce I'm swirling my cheese stick in. Staring at my food is better than looking at him, and letting him see the fear that's gripping me when it comes to Dawson. Glancing around the room, I make sure he's nowhere in sight. Which is ridiculous, unless of course he really is following me again. "I'm dealing with some issues from my past and he's being really overprotective."

"Is that why you were late to work today?" I can hear the concern dripping from his voice. As if he wants to be the one on the front lines, defending me from whatever is coming my way. But that's dumb. This is one date. Hell, not even a date. We're out drinking as friends.

"Yep," I pop the 'P.' "But I don't really want to talk about it. With any luck, everything will be taken care of soon." Then, I can move on with my life for good. I'll also make sure to pay attention to dates on court orders so I'm not blindsided again.

"Okay," he hedges. "I'm here if you want to talk

about it, though. If it becomes too serious, don't be afraid to turn to me."

My heart turns into a big puddle of goo. I can't think of a time when a guy, who isn't a part of my family, has been willing to let me voice my fears if the need arises. Hopefully it won't become an issue because the whole situation regarding Dawson is likely to scare Adrian away for good. That asshole still manages to creep into my night and ruin a perfectly good time. He's not even physically here, but the power he has is as strong as it ever was, and I need to be better at breaking that.

The bartender calls out that it's the last chance for people to get another drink. Temptation to order another one and drown out every single thought and memory of Dawson is strong. Adrian taps the table, and asks, "Are you ready to get out of here?"

"Yes." I need air and room to breathe. Is this what a panic attack feels like? If so, I don't want it.

The noise from the bar is quieting down, and I reach for my wallet. Adrian places his hand on mine. "Don't worry about it. I've got it."

He lays down a few twenties on the table, and curls his fingers around mine, helping me from my seat. This guy has to have some sort of flaw aside from his attitude at work. Nobody is this sweet without wanting some-thing more.

Outside the bar, the air is hot and sticky. Sweat already forms along my hairline, and I shiver from the drastic change in temperature. But I can breathe. There's no chance Dawson can be hanging around in a corner, waiting for his opportunity to pounce.

We walk across the street toward the parking lot beside Life in Ink. His hand still gripping mine, giving me comfort that he doesn't know I need. The only vehicle there is a motorcycle. "Where's your car?"

Smirking, he points toward the two wheeled beast. "Right there."

"Oh, hell no," I shriek. "I'm not getting on that death trap."

"Why not?" He pulls me closer to the bike. "It's perfectly safe."

"Have you not seen how many motorcycle crashes happen because the other idiots on the road don't pay attention?" Pulling my hand out of his, I cross my arms over my chest. "I'd rather not be scraped off the side of the road, thank you very much."

"I never thought you would be the scared type, Sophia." He leans against the wall beside his death machine, and sticks his hands in his pockets. "What if I promise to go really slow?"

He's mocking me. What the actual hell? Clearly, he's not in his right mind if he thinks I'm going to get on that thing. Just because I changed my entire appearance after I started working here does not mean I began doing dangerous things. I'm careful by nature. Especially now after all the crap I went through with Dawson. Getting on the back of that motorcycle does not equal a great life decision.

I'm not going to budge, and he finally realizes that. "I can call an Uber and come back for my bike if you really don't want to ride it."

He's still smiling, acting as if it's no big deal to have to pay for a ride to my place and back. My resolve wavers. I can't ask him to do that. It would be stupid, especially since he still has to drive home afterward. It's already after one in the morning. He has to be exhausted.

"I can get an Uber myself, and text you when I get home." It's not what I want to do. I'm not ready for my night with him to end. It will as soon as he drops me off because there is no way I'm inviting him in with my brother sleeping on the couch.

"Out of the question," he argues. "I told you I would take you home after drinks. It was part of the deal. We either Uber together, or I take you home on this." He pats the bike beside him.

Even though I really don't want to get on it, I can't keep myself from thinking what it would be like to have my arms wrapped around him as we drive through the city. For safety reasons, of course. "Fine," I huff, and uncross my arms. "I'll get on the stupid thing. But if I die while on the back of it, I'm coming back to haunt you for the rest of your days."

"I'll take my chances." He waves me over and pulls a helmet from somewhere on the other side of the bike. "You can wear this. It will make you feel safer; I promise."

"Where's yours?"

"Don't worry about me," he places the helmet over my head, and reaches his hand out for my purse. "I'll put this in my side bag for safe keeping. You don't want it flying off your shoulder."

"I thought you said you were going to go slow?" This is such a bad idea. Mom would lose her shit if she found out I was riding a motorcycle. She's as practical as I am, but even this would push her over the limit.

"We are," he says. "What's your address so I can put it into my gps?"

I rattle off my address as he types it into his phone. He places it in a small pouch thing between the handlebars and swings a leg over the seat. Seeing him on that motorcycle definitely increases his hotness factor. I thought he was before, but this takes it to a whole other level. Bad boys with bikes have never been my thing in the past, but that could definitely change after tonight.

"How do I get on this thing?" He has it balanced between his legs, and my mind shifts to what he would look like towering over me in bed. Get your shit together, Sophia. You will *not* attack him.

"Swing your leg over the bike, then scoot as close to me as possible, and wrap your arms around me." He says it matter of factly, but the grin on his lips says he can't wait to see how I react.

My legs are short, and it takes some work to get it over the bike. I almost fall off the other side with the momentum it takes to push my muscles to do what I need them to. Adrian's arm reaches back and steadies me before pulling me closer to him. Hesitantly, I wrap my arms around his waist, and breathe a sigh of relief. Who knew getting on a motorcycle would require so much energy?

"Are you ready?" He calls over his shoulder.

"Yes," I yell, unsure how much the helmet muffles my voice. It is so snug and padded that it blocks out some of the city noise. Inside, though, I'm terrified of becoming another traffic statistic. That would not bode well for my future.

Seconds pass and the motorcycle rumbles to life, scaring the hell out of me, and I squeeze his waist tighter. I can feel the vibration everywhere. My legs, chest, and arms. It's not quite as jarring as I become used to the sensation. But I don't let my grip on Adrian falter. He provides an attractive safety net. "Make sure to lean with me on the turns." His voice can barely be heard over the roar of the bike, but I heard him loud and clear. I will not be the reason this piece of machinery tumbles to the ground.

He pulls out onto the road, and a car pulls out from somewhere behind us moments later. I glance back, and I can't completely tell, but it kind of looks like the car from last night. I shake my head and focus on the street in front of me. It's a coincidence. Surely, Dawson wouldn't attempt to follow me when I'm with someone else. He can't be *that* obsessed. A person like him can't be taken lightly, though. As we get on the highway, I make a mental note to check back every once in a while, without letting Adrian know. He doesn't need this level of crazy tonight.

* * *

Twenty minutes later and we've arrived at my apartment complex. The car that made me anxious didn't exit when we did, and I can breathe easier knowing that we weren't being followed.

Tonight, has lasted forever, and not long enough. It's the first time I've felt normal, and like myself, than I have in ages. I would like to say it's because of Adrian's presence, but that's not the whole reason. He did put me at ease, but it felt good to go out with someone that isn't related to me. And, okay, someone who is of the male variety. Swearing myself off from dating in general after Dawson probably wasn't the smartest idea. Now I'm left not knowing what to do or how to react. Do we shake hands, hug, kiss? I'm completely out of my element here.

He stops just inside the community gate. "Which building is yours?"

"The second right turn. It's the building right on the corner." My arms have not left his body. Before it was from fear of riding. Now... it's because I don't want to let him go.

In less than a minute he's pulling into a parking space beside my car, and turning off the bike. The purr of his motorcycle cutting off brings on a deafening silence, and I'm not sure how to fill it. The complex is a ghost town at this hour. Everyone tucked into their beds not knowing that a romance could very well be forming right beneath their windows.

Adrian pushes the kickstand down before standing up to help me get off. "Be careful when you slide off. I don't want you to get burned."

"Thanks," I mumble as I awkwardly get off and fall right into his arms. Righting myself, I pull the helmet off my head, and shake my hair out. Wearing that thing makes me feel like those bobbleheads people put on their dashboards, and the having the weight taken off feels so much better.

"So," Adrian says. "Was the ride as bad as you thought it would be?"

At the word ride, an image of me on top of him flashes through my mind, and I shake it away. "Well, I didn't die. So, there's that." Taking a step closer to him, I look up into his eyes. "But it wasn't horrible."

And it wasn't. Being on the back of his bike felt free-ing. All of my problems and insecurities shedding off of me as the wind brushed past. Is it something I want to do repeatedly? That's still undecided, but next time, assuming there is one, I won't be as apprehensive about it.

"Which apartment is yours? I'll walk you to the door." He holds out his hand, waiting and hoping I'll take it. He's such a gentleman even if the attitude and motor-cycle say otherwise.

Placing my hand in his, I start toward the stairs. I've

always hated living on the second floor until now. It gives me extra time with Adrian before he rides off into the night.

Mine is all the way at the end of the landing, and the light in the living room is still on. Damn, that means Jay is still awake. Maybe I'll be lucky, and he'll have fallen asleep with everything on. Then I can prolong this moment with the man standing before me.

I push a short piece of hair that's fallen in my face behind my ear. "Thank you for tonight," I say. "It was a lot of fun. Even getting on that thing you call a vehicle."

Chuckling he moves closer to me. "I had fun, too. And that is my most cost-efficient way of getting around the city. I can bring my car next time if it will make you feel better."

Holy shit, my heart beats faster with every passing breath. He said next time. That means I didn't scare him off. Huh, I may not be as bad at this dating thing as I imagined.

"It's totally okay." I step closer. There's only a couple of inches of space between us now. "I liked it better than I thought I would." My voice sounds husky to my own ears. Did it sound like that to him? I'm not trying to be seductive, but it's hard. He makes me feel things I haven't felt in long, long time and heat consumes me.

"I'm glad." He stares into my eyes waiting for something. What, I don't know.

What do I do here? My hand is still in his. Do I wrap my arms around him for a quick hug? Or do I do what

I've wanted to do since I saw him straddling his bike? I don't let myself think about it much longer. Rising up on my tip toes, I place my lips on his, surprising him. Shit that was the wrong thing to do. I pull back, mortified. "I'm so sorry. I don't know what came over me."

Instead of calming me down, he lets go of my hand and wraps his arms around me. There isn't a part of our bodies that aren't touching. His mouth crashes into mine, and he's kissing me like I've never been kissed before. Sweet and demanding all at the time same time. His tongue pushes between my lips, and I lean into him even more, as it dances around my own.

Somewhere behind a throat clears, and I notice the sound of a television has gotten louder. "Well, well. What do we have here?"

I pull away from Adrian so quickly I almost bite his tongue, and I fall onto my brother standing behind me. "What the fuck, Jay?"

"Was I interrupting something?" He laughs. My brother is a complete asshole. So much for him being asleep.

Standing up, I glare at him. "As a matter of fact, you were, jerk."

Adrian, shockingly doesn't freak out the way I did. He straightens his shirt, and adjusts his pants. My eyes flicker down to the zipper and oh my God. It's good to know he's as interested in me as I am in him. But damn it, did Jay really have to open the door.

Adrian's eyebrows rise waiting for me to fill him in

on who the random guy in my apartment is. "Adrian," I sigh. "This is my brother, who has horrible timing by the way, Jay. Jay, this is Adrian."

Adrian stretches his arm, hand out to shake Jay's. "It's nice to meet you. I've heard a lot about you."

Jay, shakes the hand offered to him, and turns to me. "Funny, I haven't heard anything about you."

Rolling my eyes, I push Jay further inside the apartment. "I'll be inside in just a few minutes." Then, I shut the door in his face, barring him from destroying this night any further.

"Sorry about that," I lean against the door, and keep my eyes on the pavement below my feet. "He's crashing at my place for a few nights. I thought he might be asleep by now."

He places his thumb on my chin, and lifts my face up until our eyes meet. "It's okay," he whispers. "It's not exactly my finest moment to be meeting family, but it wasn't too humiliating."

"Speak for yourself," I mutter.

"Seriously, don't worry about it," he grins. "If it's okay, I'd like to do it again."

Does he mean the kiss or go on a date? I'm good with either option. Preferably both, though. I like being around him. He makes me feel safe.

Before I can offer up an answer, he kisses me on the cheek. His breath is on my ear, and I shiver. "I'll see you tomorrow at work. Goodnight, Sophia."

Without a backward glance he jogs toward the stairs.

I lean over the railing and watch him the entire way down. Once he's seated on his bike, he looks up and I give him a small wave.

Adrian will either be the best thing I need right now, or he'll be a disaster waiting to explode. But I'll take it. I'll take anything he's willing to offer me. Now, I need to pummel my brother for ruining the most amazing kiss I've ever had.

adrian

SOPHIA HAS BEEN on my mind since I dropped her off last night. Her arms wrapped around me as we drove through the city made me a lot happier than it should have. She's the first person I've ever let on my bike. Not even Miranda was able to do that. It may have taken some convincing to get her on the thing, but in the end, it worked out in my favor.

Her brother was a surprise, though. I can't help wondering if he's staying there because he's being over-protective. Not that it's a bad thing. I like that he's looking out for her, but it will dampen the moments I take her home because I'll always think he's there, watching out the window, waiting for me to completely screw up.

The smell of coffee fills the apartment, and I breathe in as much of the intoxicating scent as I can. I'm defi-nitely going to need it today after staying up late last night. Normally, I come home after work, turn on the TV and pass out before even showering. Last night, I couldn't turn my brain off. The feel of her body pressed up against mine, and the taste of her lips. The beer from the bar still present on them as I drank her in.

Groaning, I lay my head on the counter. If these thoughts of her keep up, I'm going to have to take a cold shower before going into work, and I'm already running late. I wasn't lying when I told her I look forward to going to work. I love my job. But today, I'm ecstatic to go in. Seeing Sophia after last night will be the icing on the cake. It will be hard not to sneak away to the break room every chance I get.

The coffee finally stops dripping from the machine, and I grab a travel cup to pour it into. Adding a small amount of sugar, I call it done, and walk out of the apartment. The question is... what do I take to work today? The motorcycle will give me a chance to have Sophia's arms wrapped tightly around me again. But one look at the cup in my hands, and I know I need to take the car so I have a place to set this. It's a busy day for Life in Ink, and I need to get in gear to make sure everything is set up.

* * *

Music blasts from Bianca's room as soon as I walk in. This is why we rarely have music playing in the whole shop unless Corey is here. We can never agree on what should be played. It's best to keep it to our small speakers in our own areas.

I set my coffee cup and backpack on the table in my room before walking to the break room. Charleigh is poking through the freezer, and doesn't know that I've walked in. I could be nice and let my presence be known, but I'm certain she's digging through my bag of frozen burritos. And, I can't have that. "See something you like?"

"Fuck, Adrian," she yells and tosses the bag to the back of the freezer. "You scared the shit out of me."

"Then stop pawing through my food like a starving animal." I bend down, picking up the burrito she dropped. "If you wanted one all you had to do is ask."

She yanks it out of my hand and opens it. "You weren't here, yet. And I was hoping I'd have the evidence cleared away before you came in." She shrugs her shoulders, "But I will gladly eat this one. Thank you."

"You're such a drama queen," I roll my eyes. "While you're at it, fix me a couple, too."

"You could say please," she argues.

"And you could eat your own food." I shouldn't enjoy getting under skin as much as I do, but it's hard not to. Besides, someone has to prepare her for the teen years. Jake's daughter, Layla, still has a way to go, but it will be here before she knows it.

"Point taken." She grabs two more and sets them on a plate before putting them in the microwave.

When I didn't see Sophia at the front desk, I was sure

she would be in here, putting away her lunch. Maybe I did scare her off last night, especially after she saw me readjusting my pants. What can I say? That kiss was fucking hot, and had her brother not been home, might have turned into something more. Damn, kid brothers get in the way.

The minute the microwave dings, Charleigh pulls my plate out and shoves it in my hands. It's so hot I almost drop it. "You could have let it cool down," I mutter.

"Yeah, but that would be even longer before I could put mine in. I'm getting hangry. Jake ate the last of my favorite cereal this morning."

"I guess you get a pass this one time." Grabbing a paper towel off the table, I walk back to my area and close the door. Anything to drown out Bianca's hyper music. It's too early, and I'm too tired, for that mess.

I've just finished eating when I notice Bianca's music has been turned down, and I hear Sophia. "Oh my gosh, he's such a jackass." Hopefully she's not talking about me. That would certainly deflate my ego, and make me think I imagined the spark and connection we shared last night.

Peeking out of my door, I search for the woman who plagues my thoughts. But she's not in the lobby. I don't hear her voice coming from Charleigh or Bianca's rooms either. Maybe she decided to go back home. I pick up my plate and head to the break room just in case she's in there, and this will be my excuse if she is. Not that I need one to see her, but it will make it less obvious that I've been searching her out.

Luck is on my side today. She's throwing her lunch box into the refrigerator, and wears a scowl that would make most people cower in fear. I think it's cute though. "Why are we yelling and in a bad mood this morning?"

"Ugh," she groans. "My brother."

Did he warn her away from me? If so, I'll have to talk to him. Let him now I don't have any bad intentions when it comes to his sister. Throwing my plate away, I lean against the door. "Care to elaborate?"

"He's a self-involved know it all that thinks he knows what's best for me." She picks up the pink metal cup she always brings with her and puts it under the ice maker. The ice clanks around in the cup making ping sounds until she adds the water and sits at the table.

"I take it he's not a fan of mine." My shoulders deflate, and I'm waiting for the kick to the gut similar to the blow Miranda dealt. I'm not the ideal guy to date, and not good enough.

"No, it's not that," she sighs. "Well, not entirely he's just worried about me getting my heart broken again. I haven't had the best of luck when it comes to guys."

"Is there anything I can do to ease his fears?" I genuinely want to know. Especially if it will help take away any trepidation she has as well.

"Probably not," she rolls her cup between her hands, nerves obviously taking over. "It doesn't matter anyways. I'm going to do what's best for me regardless of what he thinks. Besides, he's a lot younger than me and has no room to tell me what I should and shouldn't be doing."

While I admire her ferocity to do what makes her happy, I know how much her family means to her after hearing her talk about them last night. "You never know, he could be an old soul and handing out advice as he sees fit."

She shrugs, "Maybe. He'll always support me with whatever decisions I make. He just has a hard time with them when he's about to leave for school again. He's mostly only being the typical annoying brother, and I can't fault him for that."

That eases my fears, at least a little bit. Looks like I'm going to have to up my game to get little brother firmly on my side. The only thing I want to know now is what happened to make him feel the need to be protective of his sister in the first place. There has to be a reason, but I will wait for her to tell me in her own time. Sooner rather than later would be great, but I'm not going to push her for the information. "It's almost time for the first appointments to be rolling in. Are you sure there's *nothing* I can do to brighten your mood?"

Sophia stands and pushes her chair under the table. The screech of the chair leg scraping across the floor makes me wince. "Not really. Unless you're hiding a stash of chocolate somewhere." Her gaze is hopeful. She doesn't know me very well if she thinks I hide chocolate everywhere. I can't even stand it most of the time.

Stalking toward her, Sophia backs up until her back is flush with the wall. I place my hands right above her shoulders, and she stares at me, her mouth forming an "o" in surprise. It may be forward of me, but I meant what I said last night when I told her I wanted to do it again. I wasn't just talking about the date. "Are you sure about that?"

She shakes her head no and that's the only permission I need. Lowering my head until my lips are mere centimeters from hers, I pause savoring the effect I have on her. Her breaths are quick, and I wonder if her heart is beating at the same pace. Just before I seal my lips to hers, there's a quick intake of breath as she melts into me. I won't allow this kiss to go into panty dropping territory because we are still at work. That wouldn't be good for anybody if they happened to walk in. It's a promise for later, though.

She pulls back grinning like a Cheshire cat. "I lied. That one hundred percent put me in a better mood." The smile doesn't last long. Within seconds her brows are pinched, and she's biting on her lower lip. "Not to be a downer or anything, especially after that kiss. But what are we doing?"

Seriously, after last night and my concern over her brother not liking me, I assumed she knew where this was heading. "I kind of figured we would start dating. It's fast, I know that. But I can't get you out of my head and I want to get to know you better."

"Good," she breathed out a sigh of relief. "I thought

that's what was happening, and I just wanted to make sure." She runs her hands along the fabric of her shirt, and combs through her hair, making sure nothing is out of place. I don't know why; I never even touched her hair. If it makes her feel better though, I won't say anything. "Okay," she beams, "we should probably get out there before people, and by people, I mean Charleigh and Bianca, become suspicious."

Grabbing her hand, I give it a quick squeeze as I kiss her on the cheek before walking out of the breakroom. Who cares what Charleigh and Bianca think? What Sophia and I do isn't anybody's business unless we want it to be.

Hopefully, Sophia doesn't care what they think either. There is absolutely nothing wrong with she and I seeing each other, and I won't apologize for my feelings. The only person I can think of that might be mildly concerned is Corey, and that's because he doesn't want to lose a kick ass receptionist, or tattoo artist, should things go sour. I'll have to make sure I talk to him sooner rather than later.

* * *

So far, today has been filled with one client right after the other, leaving no time for me to see, or talk to, Sophia. Her reservations this morning have me feeling nervous. I don't want to act like some lovesick teenager, but that's how badly Sophia has me wrapped around her finger after one night of drinks. It would be different if we didn't know each other and were meeting for the first time. That's not the case, though. I've been watching her from afar, not wanting her for more than anything but a coworker. Maybe if I had approached her sooner, I wouldn't be quite so hung up on her. I only hope I don't scare her away.

"Hey, Adrian." Sophia pokes her head into my room. "I'm going to run across the street and grab some dinner. Do you want anything?"

The sound of my name on her lips is amazing, I want to hear it over and over again, preferably when we're alone and free from interruptions. "A hamburger and fries would be great."

"Alrighty, I'll be back in a little bit." She flounces out of the room before I have a chance to tell her to get some money out of my tip jar. If everything goes well with this client, and I don't have any more breaks, I might even get to eat my dinner with her.

sophia

DATING ADRIAN IS GOING to be the death of me. Especially, if he keeps starting my work days with searing hot kisses. Not that I'm complaining, but it's a little distracting. It takes me at least an hour to come out of the daze.

Bianca and Charleigh are definitely picking up on whatever lust filled vibes Adrian and I are throwing off. If I go to Adrian's workroom to talk to him, work related or not, I catch them leaning out of their doors trying to hear what we are saying. It's not that I'm trying to hide our relationship, I just don't think it's any of their business. And what if it changes my work dynamic with them, or hell even our friendship? That is not something I want to gamble with since they are the only friends I have.

"Sophia," Jay snaps his fingers in front of my face. "Stop daydreaming and listen to me."

We are sitting on opposite ends of my couch, binge

watching stand-up comedy. After we had dinner with our parents, he followed me back to my place in his own car. Even with him voicing his concerns about my dating life, my parents were ecstatic I was putting myself back out there. They basically told him to shut up and let me live my life. It's one of the few times they've taken my side against Jay. He's the baby and generally gets what he wants. Well, not this time little sibling. The parental units have my back when it comes to my happiness.

I press pause on the remote and turn toward my brother. "What were you saying?"

"I swear, you're just as bad now as you were when we were kids. You don't listen to anything I say." He crosses his arms over his chest pouting because I'm not giving him my undivided attention. He's like a little man child. Normally, I would find it adorable. Tonight, though... it's annoying as hell.

"Excuse me for putting a damper on your night." I'm not going to give in to his fit. He can either repeat what he wanted to tell me, or he can shut up and I can press play again.

Groaning, he crosses his arms and sits up straighter. "I leave for school next week. What are you going to do about Dawson? I'm not comfortable leaving you here alone when he could be following you again."

Here we go with this again. What doesn't he understand about me being able to take care of myself? I'm a quarter of a century old, and I've managed to keep myself alive thus far. "I'll keep doing what I've been doing. Walk to my car with the girls so that I'm not alone, and pay attention to my surroundings. It's not rocket science."

"Have you told Adrian about the situation with Dawson?" He has a self-satisfied smirk on his face knowing damn well I've said nothing of the sort. "I think if you *really* want to see where things go with him, you need to be honest and let him know about any possible threat."

I jump to my feet and I'm sure the person below is cussing me because of how hard I hit the floor. "We aren't even sure if he is. It's just a gut feeling, and I don't want to worry Adrian over something that may be a non-issue. "

"Better safe than sorry, Sis. Dad always says to trust your gut because it almost never lies." He leans back making himself comfortable on the couch. "Either you tell Adrian before I leave so I don't have to worry while I'm hours away, or I will tell him."

"Fine." A drink sounds really good right now. Hopefully there is still some in the back of the fridge and Jay hasn't been sneaking them. "I will tell him, but I don't want to hear any more about all of this. I'll tell him when I feel like the opportunity is right, and not when you try to work it into a conversation." He opens his mouth to argue but I cut him off. "And this means you have to give me some privacy when I'm with Adrian. All of this over-protective crap is getting old. I'm not a teenager anymore."

"Deal." Without another word he grabs the remote and presses play.

Seriously? Just like that, he is in a better mood. Freaking brat. Why couldn't my parents send him back when I begged them to? Oh well, he has a point. As much as it pains me to admit. Having him here does give me a sense of safety. I went from living with roommates in college, to moving in with Dawson, and dealing with the terror there. After that ended its fiery death, I went to my parents' before living on my own again. Most of my adult life has been sharing a house with others. It makes me question all of my life decisions. I should have been more independent. Maybe I would feel confident on my own without using my brother as a safety net.

It's a problem for another day. As much as he annoys the hell out of me, I'll miss him while he's away at school. He needs to focus on making memories, not the mess of a possible situation I've gotten myself into... yet again. For tonight, we'll laugh, confide in each other, and argue over which comedian is the best.

Bang. Bang. Bang. What in the world is going on? It sounds like someone is beating a hammer against a wall. My eyes creak open. Shards of sunlight peek through a few of the blinds that are bent at an odd angle. Ugh, I hate falling asleep on the couch. It may be comfortable, but the crick in my neck says otherwise. I'll be trying to get rid of the pain for hours. My brother could have been a gentleman and woken me up to go to bed.

The pounding comes again, and it's only then that I realize it's coming from my door. My hand reaches out toward the coffee table, knocking empty beer bottles onto the floor, in search of my phone. Finally finding it, my fingers curl around it and bring it up to my face. A few seconds pass before my eyes focus on the time. It's only nine in the morning. I groan letting my phone slip to the floor. It's way too early for this.

"Sophia." The knocks come again but was lighter this time. "Are you home?"

What the fuck is Adrian doing at my apartment this early in the morning? Even though we close early on Sundays and aren't open on Monday, I typically use this day to get in as much sleep as I can. It's also one of the few days I have to get some laundry done. Seeing him right when I wake up is something I'm not prepared for.

"Would you answer the damn door?" My brother's scratchy voice comes from somewhere on the floor. I kind of feel bad that I took his temporary bed, but he deserves it after the shit he gave me last night. And for not making me go to bed. This isn't where I planned on sleeping. "Some of us are still trying to sleep."

Opening the door would probably be the hospitable thing to do, except I can't let Adrian see me like this. At work I'm all dolled up and feel like my best self. This morning... I'm ninety percent sure I look like death warmed over. Hangovers aren't a good look on anyone.

"I'm not in any position to answer the door," I whisper loudly.

"He's going to see how you look when you first wake up eventually," Jay argues, "might as well get it over with now."

My brother obviously isn't going to save me from this situation. Where is his overprotective complex now? Because this seems like a good time for my little brother to step in and save me. Maybe if I wait a little longer Adrian will give up and go home, despite that not being what I want. Not even a little bit if my racing heart and butterflies taking flight are any indication.

The knocking stops and I wait a few moments to see if it's going to pick back up again. It doesn't, but my phone pings with the message.

Adrian: I know your home because your car is in its space.

Sophia: I'm sleeping.

Adrian: Obviously not if you're texting me back. Come open the door, I have donuts.

Adrian: With chocolate and sprinkles...

I'm definitely not one to pass on donuts, especially if chocolate is involved. That may be the only perk of him waking me up so early.

. . .

Sophia: Fine. I'm coming, but you better have a donut waiting for me as soon as I open the door.

At the sound of my feet hitting the floor my brother throws his arm up in victory. "Finally, maybe I can go back to sleep now."

"Oh, shut up," I throw a pillow at him. He grunts as it hits him in the face, and it's my turn though my hands up in the air in victory. "If you really want to go back to sleep, go climb in my bed."

He doesn't argue. With a blanket in hand he stumbles his way down the hall and into my room before shutting the door firmly behind him.

I rub my eyes to make sure they are clear of any sleep. It's the best I can do on short notice. He's definitely not getting beauty queen material right now. My walk toward the door resembles a zombie trying to find its way toward brains.

"Well aren't you a ray of sunshine," Adrian laughs as I open the door.

"Nope," I hold out my hand. "I was promised a donut, and yet there isn't one in my hand."

He sets the chocolate donut, with sprinkles, in my waiting hand. I don't say thank you, or any of that, because I'm too busy shoving the donut in my mouth. Leaving the door open I walk to the couch and make myself comfortable. "I'll have to remember that you aren't a morning person," Adrian says as he shuts the door.

"Not even a little bit," I mumble through my mouth full of food. "It doesn't help with the late night. I'd still be sleeping, at least until noon, had you not been banging on my door."

Adrian winces at my comment. "Sorry, next time I will call before I show up." He looks awkward standing in the middle of my living room, completely lost like he doesn't know what to do. His eyes are everywhere but on me, studying his surroundings and trying to get a better picture of who I am as a person. He isn't going to get much because of the sparse decorations. I haven't had much time, or the will, to do add things to the wall. A year later and I'm still trying to figure out who I am as a person.

"You know you can sit down, right?" I pat the seat next to me on the couch. "Just because I'm grouchy doesn't mean I'm going to bite. Besides, you still have the donuts and you are *way* over there. How am I supposed to reach the box?"

He stares at me warily. "Promise you won't bite?" He takes a few cautious steps closer to me. "Not that I would mind, I just don't want to lose a hand because I woke you up. Where's your brother? I thought he was staying with you." He looks around the room as if Jay is going to pop up out of nowhere. That might actually be kind of funny.

"He's about as happy as I am about the early morning wake up call, so I sent him to my room to get the rest of his beauty sleep." Now that all of his attention is focused on me, I feel nervous. My hair is most likely sticking up in all directions, and I run my fingers over it attempting, and most likely failing, to calm it down.

Judging by the shit eating grin on Adrian's face, I don't think it's working. This is why showing up unannounced is a horrible idea. If you are excited to see that person, there's a chance you will see them when they aren't looking their best and end up giving them a complex. This isn't a first day of dating look I have going on. This normally happens after being together for a bit. Adrian places his hand over mine keeping me from fretting with my hair. "You look fine, Sophia."

Groaning, I shake my head, "I'm not sure what your definition of fine is but this isn't it."

"You're beautiful no matter how you look." He's staring into my eyes, hell into my soul, and I feel each word as he says them.

The compliment puts me at ease. The whole time I was with Dawson, I had to look picture-perfect and it's hard to get away from that mentality when it comes to somebody I'm interested in. Instead of showing any sort of reaction to his words, I change the subject "So are you just going to hang on to those donuts, or are you going to share them?"

Adrian scoots back enough to make room for the box of donuts. He doesn't take one, but gestures for me to get whatever I want. There's a plastic bag sitting on the floor beside him that I didn't even notice until he pulls it up into his lap. "I wasn't sure what you like to drink with your breakfast," he pulls out four bottles. "So, I got a little bit of everything."

Next to the box he sets down chocolate milk, strawberry milk, water, and orange juice. "I think regular milk feels left out. How can you get all the other kinds and not get that one?"

He shudders, "I don't see how anybody can bring themselves to drink regular milk. It's boring and has a weird aftertaste. The only acceptable way to drink it is with a ton of either chocolate or strawberry syrup." He nods matter-of-factly, as if he has to get the point across to me.

"I'll take the..." I tap my finger on my chin acting like I'm deep in thought. "Orange juice."

"Then why were you giving me shit about the milk?" He scrunches his nose up. It's actually kind of adorable.

He had a point about the milk but I don't even like it with the extra syrup and stuff. "Because you woke me up at an ungodly hour. It's only fair that I give you crap about whatever I want. Next time, you'll call. Or better yet, let me sleep in."

He sets the bottles I didn't choose on the coffee table. "You're kind of cute when you're moody," he chuckles.

"The only reason I let you in is because you have food," I shrugged. "And maybe because you're a little hot. Otherwise, I would have let you stay outside until you gave up and left."

"You think I'm hot?" He leans closer going in for a

kiss. This is not good. Normally it wouldn't be a problem, but just no.

That's not going to happen yet. I put up my hand in defense, "I haven't even brushed my teeth. You're not kissing me. That's gross."

He's on the verge of arguing when Jay's voice fills the room. "Are those donuts?" He's just short of skipping to the couch, and plops himself down beside me. Reaching around me to grab a delicious pastry, he asks, "So what's on the agenda for today? I don't want to be stuck in this apartment."

And this is the beginning of the end of my brother. So much for taking a backseat and not intruding. Siblings can be so annoying.

adrian

HAVING Sophia's little brother tag along with us all day is not what I had in mind when I showed up to her door this morning with breakfast. I'm not going to dwell on the negative though. I'll use this chance to prove to her brother that I genuinely like her, and I want to see where things go. If things go my way, we'll be great friends by the time we make it back to her house.

"Yo, Adrian," Jay yells at me. "You're up. Or, I could always bowl for you."

We ended up at a bowling alley that also has miniature golf and laser tag. It was the only thing I could think of that would entertain all three of us, and provide enough opportunities for Sophia and I to sneak away. "I'm coming, I'm coming. I'm ahead of both of you, and I don't want to lose my top spot."

He rolls his eyes and sits down on one of the benches in front of the lane. "I'm not that bad."

Sophia is laughing so hard she has her hands wrapped around her stomach. "Dude, you're pretty bad if even I am winning against you. And we all know how much I suck at bowling."

Seeing their bond makes me long for my family. Even though they aren't supportive, the camaraderie that these two have with their family is refreshing. It's a pipe dream, though, and never likely to happen. I haven't talked to them in years and I don't see that changing anytime soon. If they decide to stop being so damn judgmental one day, I'll consider opening up to them again.

"What is this? Pick on Jay day." He glares at his big sister but he doesn't mean it. The small smile playing on his lips an indication that he's only joking. "Go ahead and prove how awesome you are, Adrian. After this, though, I want to go play laser tag. There's no way in hell either of you are going to be any good at that."

Sophia snorts, "Just because you wasted away your summers playing video games doesn't mean you're going to be any good at laser tag."

"Those are the words of someone who is scared." He puffs his chest out to make himself look bigger. "Don't worry, I'll go easy on you."

I pick up one of the balls from the return and almost drop it on my foot. Their bickering is comical and it is hard to hold in my laughter. "I almost want to bow out of the game just so I can see you to go at it. Who knows, maybe I can be a judge."

"There's no need for that," Jay waves me away. "It's a

point system, and you get points for every target you hit." It's silent for a few seconds. "Let's make this interesting." He says it just as I release the ball and it goes into the gutter. I'm curious how he's going to make a game of laser tag interesting. Cursing at my bad throw, I face the both of them.

"You're on," Sophia shifts until one of her legs is bent beneath her. "What are the terms?"

I rush to stand between them, and hold up my hand. "Is this really necessary? I feel like you two are about to come to blows."

"Oh, it's nothing physical," Jay assures me. "If my score is more than both of yours combined, y'all pay for the pizza. But if you beat me, the food is on me."

Sophia reaches around me and pushes her brother. So much for not getting physical. How the hell did I become the adult in this situation? My level of expertise in sibling fights is exactly zero. "How are you even going to pay? You don't have a job."

"That doesn't mean I don't have money," he cuts in, "but... if you're too scared, I'll take my pizza now."

"There are only two more frames left in this game," Sophia sits up straighter. "After this we," she points between herself and me, "are going to kick your ass."

"Bring it on big sister, let's see what you've got." With the gauntlet thrown down, Jay picks up one of the bowling balls and sends it soaring down the lane. I'm unsure whether he knows that it's still my turn, but I don't say anything. "You're welcome for knocking down the rest of your pins." Well, that answered my question. "Guess I don't suck as bad as y'all thought."

Laser tag is a lot harder than it appears. It is pitch black except for a few black lights covering the obstacles throughout the room. All of the players have neon reflective strips on their vests dividing us into two teams. You would think spotting the other players would be easy, but the way they weave around and dodge under the structures placed around the room is ridiculous. I'm pretty sure a lot of these people play more often than others, and I feel like a complete newbie.

One of the players on my team bumps into my shoulder and whispers, "I think that guy over there is gunning for you." He's not wrong. Jay has managed to find me no less than ten times in the fifteen minutes we have been in here. If he's going to be around us a lot, or we do things like this again, I'm going to have to get better on my laser tag skills because this isn't cutting it. He's going to make fun of me every chance he gets.

"Thanks man," I say much louder than a whisper and the light on my vest flashes red once again.

* * *

Taking the vest off is such a relief. I'm hot, sweaty, and I'm sure I look like complete shit. This has to be what

Sophia felt like earlier, and I feel kind of bad for not giving her warning before just going to her house. It's not that I don't think she's beautiful when she first wakes up, but she had this fear in her eyes as she was trying to brush her hair with her fingers. Obviously, she's not used to people showing up unannounced, and I shouldn't have put that burden on her.

Sophia pulls her vest off like the material is burning her skin. "Hurry up, Adrian. I want to go see what the final scores are." I never realized how much of a competitive streak she has in her, and it will definitely make for some fun interactions in the future. My mind is already spinning with things I can challenge her with.

Both her and Jay are standing in front of two monitors when I join them outside the laser tag area. Jay has a horrified expression on his face while Sophia's arms are crossed, smug.

"I take it we're not buying pizza?" The shock on Jay's face is hysterical. It's exactly what he gets for thinking that he could be better than us without even knowing if we can play. Well, Sophia can actually play because let's face it I sucked it up in there, and it will be surprising if I got any points.

"Nope," Sophia beams. "Pizza will be on my lovely brother because he obviously underestimated me."

"I don't understand," Jay mumbles, "that should have been an easy win for me, but these old people somehow managed to beat me. It's just not possible."

My head snaps back, "Who are you calling old?

You're only as old as you feel, and I still feel like I'm in my teens." I waggle my eyebrows at Sophia, and she's barely holding in her laughter.

She opens her mouth, no doubt to rub our victory in a little bit more, when her phone rings. Pulling it out of her back pocket she checks the screen and all the color drains from her face. She accepts the call and walks away from us trying to find a quiet place to take it. I'm curious what the call is about, and why it has her so shaken up. I don't think I earned the right to ask yet, soon though.

Sophia shakes her head as she walks toward us. Her eyes hold a hint of fear and anger, and whatever news she just received isn't what she was hoping for. Jay rushes over to her before she makes it back and they share a heated argument in whispers. He nods his head toward me, and my stomach sinks. Maybe he's trying to warn her off of me again despite what she wants.

"Is everything okay?" I ask as she steps beside me and leans into my side. The fact that she is near me and Jay isn't saying anything is enough to wipe my fears away. At least for now.

Sighing she puts her head on my shoulder, "Yeah. I just got some news that I'm not all that thrilled about."

"Can I help with anything?" Sophia's already shaking her head no before the question is fully out of my mouth.

"There isn't really anything you can do." She's pulling away from me and my heart pounds at the lack of contact. Wondering if she's going to let go completely. Ugh, I hate this. It's been well over a year since I ended things with Miranda, and my insecurities of something better pulling attention away from the relationship still plague me.

Jay opens his mouth and Sophia glares at him. He doesn't pay her any attention, "Actually, there is."

"Why do I get the feeling there's something you're not telling me?" If she is in some sort of danger, and it sounds like she might be, I'll do anything I can to protect her. I can't do that unless she tells me what is going on, though.

"Soph, now is probably a good time to tell him." Jay is facing his sister, eyes pleading for her to open up to me. "You dealt with it alone last time. You don't have to do it again." He points toward me, as if I'm some sort of saving grace for her.

I am completely lost now, and I'm hoping one of them can clear things up for me. As much as I want to see where things go with Sophia, I also don't want to be mixed up in some unknown drama. "Can either of you explain to me what exactly is going on?" I don't mean to sound exasperated, but I can't help it. They are talking around something and I don't like being left in the dark.

"This isn't really a place I want to discuss it." Sophia's eyes are on mine, asking for understanding. "Why don't we grab a pizza to go because J still owes us, and I will tell you everything."

She has a point, I guess. There are people everywhere in this place, and if it is something extremely personal, standing outside of a laser tag room probably isn't the best location.

"I can respect that," I put her fear at ease. "But I want to know *everything*, no withholding information."

"Deal." She grabs my hand and shakes it. Even when she's completely freaking out, she manages to do something so innocent, it makes me laugh.

"Could you drive any slower?" Jay whines from the back seat. "I'm hungry, and if we don't get home soon, I'm going to eat it straight out of the box. Nasty ass pineapple or not."

"So, you think the pineapple thing is weird too?" We're in Sophia's car since I rode my bike to her apartment. How she slept through the noise of that thing is beyond me. He's not wrong about her driving, though. If I had to guess, she's trying to take as long as possible to get back to her apartment to avoid telling me what's happening with her. It's not going to work. I can be very persistent.

"Y'all really shouldn't knock the pineapple until you've tried it." She glances at her brother in the rearview mirror. "It's life changing."

"So is skydiving," Jay snorts, "but you don't see me strapping a tiny piece of fabric onto my body and jumping out of a perfectly good plane."

My stomach grumbles, and I'm with Jay on her

needing to speed up. "I've seen you drive, Sophia. I know you can go faster than this, and I'm getting... what did Charleigh call it? Oh, yeah, hangry." I point to my stomach, emphasizing my point.

"Fine." She rolls her eyes. She steps on the gas pedal harder and turns up the radio to block out mine and Jay's complaining.

sophia

MY PALMS ARE SWEATING, and I'm ten times more nervous than I was when I went on the "sort of" date with him last week. It's not that I don't *want* to tell Adrian about the issues I've had in the past with Dawson. I just don't want him to break up with me because of the extra drama. From what I've seen, guys don't do drama.

Both Adrian and Jay are too busy shoveling food into their mouths to demand information. Even Jay doesn't know what the call was about, not completely. He only knows that things didn't work out in my favor.

Grabbing a slice of my ham and pineapple pizza, I take a huge bite. Adrian looks at the pizza in disgust. "There's no way that is good on any level."

"You could always try it," I hold the piece out toward him.

"Will that get me answers faster?" So much for him possibly forgetting about the talk we need to have.

"Probably not," I shrug, "but you might like it…"

"Then I'm good." He sets the crust of his pizza on the plate in front of him. That's weird to me. Why not eat the whole thing? I don't say anything, though. Unlike him, I don't question other people's food choices. "So, what was the phone call about?"

"Wow," I mutter, "just jump right in. No warm up or small talk to build up to it."

"I like to be straight forward. It helps in the long run." Pain flashes through his eyes, and I wonder if it was another person who put it there. Instinctively, I want to reach out, grab his hand, and comfort him. Whatever caused that pain must have hit him hard.

I don't do any of that, though. Hell, I don't know if I can touch him at all while revisiting the insanity my life was before I broke free. "Do you want me to start with the call or from the beginning?"

My brother doesn't say anything, but he moves closer to me for support. Knowing that he saw me when I was at my absolute lowest kills me inside, but I'm happy he's seen how far I've come from being *that* girl. Reinvention and everything, it was what I needed to become the best version of myself. I'm still not where I want to be, though.

"Start with the phone call, and then go back," Adrian grabs my hand. "If it gets to be too much, you don't have to tell me everything."

This man, who seemed like he never cared about me before, is doing all the right things to ease my fear. It's the only reason I'll tell him everything, even if it hurts. "Well, the day I came in late, I had just finished trying to file a restraining order. The officer told me he'd be in contact with me when, and if, a hearing was set." Deep breath in, long exhale. This is the part that Jay doesn't know either. "That was him who called. The judge didn't sign off on a hearing because of lack of proof."

Jay lowers his head in defeat, but Adrian's grip on my hand loosens the tiniest bit. "Wait," he says, "who were you filing a restraining order on?"

"Her ex-boyfriend," Jay supplies, "he's a douchebag of the highest level. I didn't care for him when they were together, and I hate him a little more since she left him."

"How long ago did you end things with him?" Even though his grip isn't as strong, his hand is still over mine, and that brings me some comfort.

"About four months before I started working at Life in Ink."

"And he's still bothering you?" Adrian's brows are furrowed. He has every right to be confused. Honestly, I am too.

"He hasn't for a long time, but I didn't know that restraining orders expire. And a car seemed to be following me home last week. It creeped me out. I have a gut feeling he's back now that the original order is no longer valid."

"I don't understand why he would come back to bother you after all this time," Jay mutters.

"Is he a threat to you?" Adrian scoots closer to my side, trying to calm the shaking he no doubt feels in my hands. "Was he abusive toward you?"

"He was never physical," I answer. It's not easy to talk about, even now. "But he was verbally abusive and manipulative. He would twist my words to make me look like an idiot when he was being an asshole with a God complex."

"What happened when you left him?" So many questions in such a short amount of time. I guess I should thank my lucky stars he isn't running, screaming, out of the front door. It does little to push my fears away, though.

"I tried sneaking out during the night, and I was shocked he let me go without a fight when he woke up as I was walking out." I honestly thought it was over. I wouldn't have to deal with him ever again. Boy was I wrong. "He started showing up at my parents' house at all times of the day, and constantly calling my phone. There were a few times I went out by myself and he'd show up wherever I was." That was the scariest part. Never knowing if he would torment me in front of people. "After that happened, my dad took me to the police station to get a restraining order put on him. Luckily, he documented each occurrence so it wasn't an issue. After testing our patience on if we would make him stick to it, he backed off completely."

Adrian is silent beside me, taking in all the information I just threw at him. He said he wanted to know everything, and that's what I gave him. Fingers crossed he doesn't regret asking me out for drinks. "Is it possible that he never actually stopped following you? He only got better at not being spotted?"

"It's crossed my mind a few times," I answer. The times I'd be walking down the road, and the hair on the back of my neck would stand up... those are the times I felt his presence without seeing him.

"Are you serious right now, Soph?" Jay butts in. "Why didn't you say anything if you suspected it?"

"Because you, Mom, and Dad finally had some sort of peace when things calmed down. You had your road trip, and they needed a break from constantly worrying about me."

"You should have let us decide how much we wanted to pile onto our plates," he's sitting on the floor a few inches from the couch. Bumping my leg with his shoulder he adds, "Family first. That's the way it's always been, and always will be. We get to decide what's important enough to protect. And you will *always* be at the top of that list."

He's the reason I've been forced to have this conversation with Adrian. It warms my heart to know he feels that way, though. Most siblings spend their entire life bickering and fighting for attention, but Jay has my back whenever I need him. I've done the same for him, and will continue to do so. There may be times when I feel like my family is *too* involved with my life, and it drives me bonkers. They only do it because they love me, though. It took me being treated like shit by the man that was supposed to love me to come to my senses. To find my way back to what is important to me.

"I'm with Jay," Adrian pipes in. "You should have told them. On the other hand, I understand why you didn't." He pulls me into him and I almost kick Jay in the head, earning me a middle finger. "I won't let anything happen to you, though. If this guy is a problem, I'll help you collect any proof you need. You have a support team around to make sure you're safe."

"Thanks. I appreciate that," I mumble into his chest. "I'm shocked you're still willing to stick by me with all the craziness."

"As long as you want to be with me, and aren't using me for anything, I'm in." He presses a kiss on top of my head. "I told you before, I really like you, and I want to see what happens."

Laughing, I lean further into him. "I've liked you for a lot longer than you liked me. Even when I knew it was a bad idea after all the crap with Dawson. I needed to learn how to be my own person before I allowed myself to have feelings for someone else. It didn't quite work out that way."

"I'm happy it didn't. I've been interested in you since the day you walked into Life in Ink to get your first tattoo."

"The two of you realize you're not alone, right?" My

brother's voice comes from the kitchen. I didn't even notice him leave the room. "While I appreciate your willingness to help keep Dawson away from her, if he is in fact, back to make her life hell... this love fest is making me sick to my stomach." He grabs his stomach, acting like he's about to vomit.

"You do have a perfectly fine room of your own at Mom and Dad's," I argue. "If being here makes you feel nauseated, you can always leave."

"But you have the pizza," he pouts.

"Take it with you," I huff. "It's the least you can do after completely going against the deal we made."

"What deal?" Adrian asks.

"That he'd let me tell you about Dawson when I thought the time was right. Instead," I point finger in Jay's direction, "the jackass practically forces me to tell you."

"I'm happy you told me," Adrian says, sweeping a piece of hair behind my ear. "I was burned pretty badly before because we weren't on the same page. I don't want that to happen with us. Honesty is always the best policy, even when you don't think it's a big deal."

"I was going to tell you," I whine. "Just not quite so soon. I wanted to determine whether it was a true threat or not."

Jay picks up the box containing the pepperoni pizza. "While I would love to sit here and listen to y'all argue, or be all sickeningly romantic." He opens his mouth and mimes making himself sick, "I'm going home. Not for good," he eyes me, knowing inside I'm throwing a victory party. "Just long enough for the two of you to do whatever you want. I know me being here is cramping your style."

"Why are you still here?" I groan. "Leave already," I throw a pillow at him. "I'll call you when you can come back."

"I plan on sleeping here tonight," he argues.

"Not if I don't call you, you aren't." Adrian smirks at his insistence. "Stay away until I call you."

"Fine," he spits out. "I can tell when I'm no longer welcome."

"Whatever," I roll my eyes. "Are you tired of sleeping on the couch anyway?"

"You have a point," he nods. "I'll await your call, fair sister." He bows, grabs his keys, and he's gone within seconds.

Finally, he's not around to make things awkward between me and Adrian. Now, I can get to know him without an audience. It looks like my day is already brightening.

adrian

JAY HASN'T BEEN BACK to Sophia's in three days much to his dismay. The small bit of freedom he felt last week has been snatched from him. I should feel bad about being selfish with her since he leaves for school this weekend, but I don't. The upside is at least he knows that she is safe with me.

The nights I've been at her apartment could definitely be more exciting. I don't want to take advantage of her situation, though. Instead of trying to crawl into bed with her, I've been a perfect gentleman and sleeping on the couch. How in the world does Jay sleep on this thing? While it's the perfect size for Sophia's small stature, it does nothing for anyone who is tall. My feet either hang off the edge or I'm sitting up while trying to sleep. It's almost as frustrating as not being curled up with the woman who stays on my mind more than she should.

There are still a few more hours before we have to

head to work, and I grab the two blankets I'm using and lay them out on the floor. I'm betting it would be slightly more comfortable even though it is hard as a rock beneath the cheap carpet. Finally, I lie down with way more space to move, maybe I can get some actual sleep.

My eyes are closed, and I'm in that weird space where you're just about to fall asleep but not quite there yet when I hear Sophia. "Adrian?"

"Yeah," my voice is husky and it sounds like I've been smoking for years, even though I haven't.

"Where are you?" I can imagine her looking everywhere around the room, trying to pinpoint my location.

Apparently, I will not be getting any sleep this morning. It's going to make for a *very* long day. "Down here."

"Why are you on the floor?" She's staring down at me, hair sticking up in all directions. Looks like she stopped being so self-conscious about her looks first thing in the morning. I'm not complaining one bit. She's adorable when she first wakes up.

I raise my hand and point toward the couch. "I don't fit on that thing, and I was tired of having to turn into a contortionist to try to make it happen. The floor seemed like a better option."

She sits on the floor next to me, legs crisscrossed. "You could've slept in my bed, silly. There is plenty of room." It's so innocent when it comes out of her mouth, while my intentions would have been anything but that.

"Then your virtue would have been at stake." I roll from my side to my back so I can get a full view of her.

Sophia laughs and places her hand on my abs. "People actually still use that word? It's so old-fashioned." She begins walking her fingers toward my chest, and I'm really beginning to regret this blanket covering me. "Besides, my virtue is the least of my concerns."

Shit, I hope she doesn't look down. She'll see a tent in the blanket, and just how much those words turn me on. Mind out of the gutter, Adrian. Her comment wasn't a double entendre. Was it?

"Oh," my voice cracks and my cheeks flame with embarrassment. Ugh, will this woman ever stop making me feel like a teenage boy? Clearing my throat, I try again, "What are your most pressing concerns?"

She glances down and her eyes widen. Fuck, this is so embarrassing. "Um." Her pale cheeks turn bright pink, and at least I know I'm not alone in the torment. She's affected as much as I am. "Jay is throwing a fit about being stuck at our parents' house. He says Mom gives him no privacy and it's my fault because you're staying with me. Plus, they are throwing him a going away party this weekend."

Nice subject change on her part. "Why is this party a concern?"

Snorting, she shakes her head. "Oh honey," she pats my chest. "It's not one for me. It is for you, though. You've been invited and are expected to show up. My parents want to meet you. I already told them you would be there."

Anxiety isn't something I've ever dealt with, but now it's showing its ugly head. There's nothing like mentioning parents to diffuse any naughty thoughts that were playing inside my head. "Do I have to meet your parents?"

"Yup." She stands up and walks toward the kitchen. "Unless you want to be considered as Dawson two point zero, it would be in your best interest to come along and deal with whatever questions they throw at you."

It can't be that bad. Not if they've raised Sophia and Jay to be the smartass people they are. If they are even a fraction of their parents, I think we might get along great. "Wait, why would they compare me to Dawson?"

"Because," her voice floats to me from the kitchen, "he never wanted to be around them. And, when he was... he did his best to be a huge douchebag and constantly implied he was better than them. They were never fans of his, and I wish they'd spoken up about it. Not that it would have mattered." She mutters the last statement, but it's loud enough I can hear it.

"We can't have that now, can we?" I throw the blanket off of me before remembering my morning situation, and wrap it around my waist as I stand up. "From what I've heard of him, I'm the total opposite of Dawson." I find her in the kitchen and wrap my arms around her, placing a chaste kiss on her shoulder. "Your parents are going to love me."

* * *

Nope, I *do not* want to do this. Meeting the parents is a big step considering we've just started dating. It's worth it, though. At least that's what I keep repeating inside my head.

Luckily, Raven was my only appointment this evening and was okay with rescheduling. She had a last-minute work event, and told me to "go knock the socks off of my lady friend's parents." I'm not entirely sure that is going to happen, but I'll give it my best shot.

Being off early on Friday night is weird, and I can't remember the last time that's happened. Miranda was always mad at me because of my weekend schedule. The fact that I never once took off on a weekend for her, but I'll do it for Sophia without batting an eye speaks volumes. My connection with her is something I've never felt before, and it gets stronger with each passing day.

My apartment feels foreign to me since I've been crashing at Sophia's place. The air is stale when I walk in even though the air conditioner has been running the entire time I've been away. Where her apartment is mismatched and cozy, mine is modern and has a sense of sterility. I used to love my apartment, but without the person I want most, I don't even want to be here.

The first thing I need to figure out is what to wear. I don't want them thinking I'm trouble for Sophia. Most people see others with tattoos and think they are nothing but trouble. Sophia has tattoos, though. They still talk to her, and treat her with respect. At least I assume they do since she has nothing but good things to say about them.

My room would give teenage girls a run for their money. There are clothes piled on my bed and thrown on the floor in my search for the perfect outfit. I have to pick Sophia up in an hour, and I'm still not dressed. The long sleeve button up shirts are out. It's way too damn hot for that, even if it may give off a good impression. Short sleeve button ups make me look weird. Miranda bought them for me, and I really need to donate them since they aren't my style.

In the end I choose a white T-shirt and jeans. It's the most comfortable and I won't have embarrassing sweat stains at any point during the night. Nothing says give me a hug like sweaty pits. Now, on to the shoes. I own more Converse and Vans than any person has a right to. Should I go for fun, or classic?

My gaze roams over the many shoe racks along the bottom half of my closet, hoping a pair grabs my attention. So far, nothing. My Doc Martens are right beside the door, but they are incredibly heavy when you wear them for a long period of time. I have no clue what this party will be like, or if there will be plenty of chairs to take a break from the weight on my feet. Maybe I'm being over dramatic about the whole thing, who cares? Aching feet are never a good thing, and the Docs are nixed without a second thought. One more sweep across the rows of shoes, and I settle on classic checker patterned Vans. It matches what I'm wearing, and my feet won't hate me in the morning.

Thirty minutes later, I'm pulling into Sophia's apartment complex. She gave me the option to just go to her parents' house, but I'm not that brave. I need some sort of buffer, and it will put me at ease if she introduces me rather than showing up and making a complete ass of myself.

I park next to her car, and sigh in relief when I don't see Jay's car. Looks like I'll get some time alone with her before I face the firing squad. Taking the steps two at a time, I'm at her door in less than a minute. Jay answers the door. I guess there's no alone time after all.

"Why so glum?" Jay asks, opening the door wider to let me in.

"It doesn't matter," I mutter.

"It's me isn't it?" He grins. "There will be no hanky panky before my big party. It's my day, and I will not have my big sis showing up late with her hair in disarray."

"You're disgusting," Sophia pushes her brother out of the way. "What Adrian and I do with our time is none of your business." She shoots me a wicked smile and winks. "Hell, we could go to my room right now, your presence in my apartment be damned."

"Oh my God, I think I actually threw up in my mouth." He rolls his eyes, "Yet I'm the disgusting one."

Sophia shrugs then launches herself into my arms. "I missed you," she whispers in my ear.

"It's only been a day," I chuckle, and pull her closer.

"That's too long." She places her lips on mine, and kisses me as if it's going to be the last time. I deepen the kiss, tongue sliding between her lips and I can taste the cider she's been drinking. My tongue massages hers. She grips me tighter and moans.

"You have a fucking audience," Jay yells. "Can you not do that in front of me?"

Sophia pulls away from me, wiping around her lips to make sure her lipstick hasn't smudged. It has, but I'm not going to tell her. She looks hot as hell right now, and I want to skip the party altogether. "Then go to Mom and Dad's."

"I don't have my car," he argues.

"You can take mine," she bites back. "It's not like you've never driven it before."

"And how will you get there?" He asks like he's won this battle.

She waves at me, "In case you haven't noticed, my boyfriend is standing right here and perfectly capable of giving me a ride over there. We're going to the same place." Referring to me as her boyfriend makes me want to puff out my chest. I'm proud to be her boyfriend, and there's nothing that can change that.

"No dice, Sis," he pouts. "I don't trust that you'll show up. It's not like I'll be here forever or anything. Come Sunday I'll be hundreds of miles away, and will not be gracing you with my presence."

"You are such a baby. Fine, we'll stop and all ride to

your party together. Will that make you happy?" She attempts to look angry with a scowl, but the quirk of her lips says otherwise. She's going to miss her brother when he's away at college. I'll make sure to keep her occupied, though.

Giving her hand a squeeze, I pull her to my side. "Are y'all ready? We can head over early."

"Are you that excited to meet my parents?" Sophia looks up at me with a small smile.

"Not really," I shake my head. "But I might as well get it over with. How bad could it be?"

The sudden joy on Jay's face has me worried, and I want to take back everything I just said. This is going to be awkward; I can already tell.

sophia

I'M NOT sure who is more nervous, Adrian or me. I wasn't lying when I said my parents hated Dawson. This whole meeting could go one of two ways... they love him and envelop him into our family. Or, they loathe him and want me to dump him as quickly as possible. The both of them are a lot more outspoken after the Dawson bullshit.

"Where do I turn?" Adrian looks in both directions at the stoplight before the street my parents live on. He's trying to play it cool, but his thumbs haven't stopped drumming the steering wheel since we left my place. The drive isn't long, and I want to give him shit about driving less than the speed limit. It's only fair since him and Jay did it to me earlier this week. I don't want to add to his nerves so I won't say anything.

"The next street on the left," I point toward it. "You'll go around a corner and the house is on the right."

He nods, pressing the gas pedal as the light turns

green. He's going to have to speed up a bit because the lights in this area change fast. "Are you ready to head back to school?"

The question comes out of nowhere, and it takes a few moments for Jay to respond. "Yes, and no. I'm happy to be away from my helicopter parents for a while," he glares at me as if this is my fault. Okay, maybe it is a little. If I would have gone to them when Dawson and I were first having problems, a lot of my problems could have been avoided. "I miss being home sometimes, though. Do you have any idea how much of a pain in the ass it is to lug laundry up and down flights of stairs?"

"Actually, yeah," Adrian laughs. He pulls behind the long line of cars in front of the house. "The first apartment I had didn't have a washer or dryer, and I was on the third floor. I'd have to go to the closest laundromat, and carrying my clothes up and down was ridiculous. It would have helped if I didn't wait so long between trips."

When Jay doesn't respond, Adrian shifts the car into park. A few moments pass and Jay opens the door. "Well, I'll see y'all in there."

Adrian places his hand on the key, but doesn't turn the car off. "Are you okay?" He's being weird, and I don't know what to make of it.

He shrugs, not meeting my face. "Kind of. Meeting parent hasn't exactly gone smoothly for me."

"What do you mean?" Once you get past his broody exterior, Adrian is an amazing guy. He's kind, funny, and one hell of a kisser. Any parent would be happy to have him dating their daughter. I have no doubt mine will love him.

He removes his hands from the key and takes off his seatbelt. Slowly shifting his body until he's facing me, his gaze meets mine. "My last girlfriend, well fiancée, was mortified about how I chose to dress when I met her parents. It wasn't anything horrible, but it wasn't super dressy either." How did I not know he had a fiancée? It seems like that is something he would've told me whenever I told him about Dawson. Or, at least he should have. Now isn't the time to grill him about it though. "She was terrified how I would appear to her parents, and holy shit she was right to be. Her dad took one look at me and wrote me off as not good enough."

"Adrian," I place my hand over his in solidarity, wishing I could take all of his nerves and worry and throw them out the window. "I can guarantee you my parents aren't like that. I mean, look at me. Since I started working at Life in Ink, I've used my body as a canvas. If they were judgmental assholes, they would have disowned me a long time ago." Pulling his hand to my lips, I kiss his inked knuckles. "The only thing they care about is your character, how you treat me, and if you make me happy."

He leans over the center console, leans his forehead against mine, and places his free hand on my cheek. "Are you sure?"

"Absolutely. You have, in my opinion, checked off all three things. Believe me, they are happy you've been watching out for me. You have nothing to worry about." I tilt my head until my lips meet his. Parting his lips with my tongue I show him just how happy he makes me.

His fingers entwine in my hair and he grips it, bringing me as close to him as possible in our awkward position. This kiss could be a lasting seconds, minutes, or an eternity. All I know is I can feel him pouring all of himself into me. His fears, anxiety, and a promise to stand by my side. Our feelings are escalating at such a fast pace, but I relax into him knowing it goes both ways. He pulls back slowly, smoothing my hair down and whispers, "Thank you." He undoes my seatbelt and turns off his car. "I think I'm ready now."

Old country music blasts through the Bluetooth speakers Dad has set up around the yard. Adrian scrunches up his nose in disgust at the sound as we pass through the side gate into the backyard. "What's the matter?" I bump into him with my hip. "You don't like this kind of music?" It's not my cup of tea, either. The difference is I've learned to tune it out since I grew up on it.

He lifts the hand not holding mine and rubs the back of his neck. "It's not exactly my first choice. But it looks like Jay doesn't care for it either." He points to my little brother, face stricken in horror. He keeps looking from his friends to our parents in disbelief. He deserves it after being a total buzzkill earlier by not driving my car. I get it, though, he's going to be gone until Thanksgiving. He's going to miss me. He better, anyway.

Mom and Dad have shit eating grins on their faces and are giggling like school kids. Leave it to them to mess with my brother on his last weekend home. "They are just screwing with him," I whisper to Adrian. "They take every advantage possible to embarrass us."

"Oh yeah," he lifts an eyebrow. "Now I can't wait to meet them."

"Just know that whatever they tell you is an absolute lie." My hand grips his, and I pull him toward my parents. There's no better time like the present to get this meeting over with. He may be cussing me in his head right now, and that's alright. Once we say hello to Mom and Dad, all the awkwardness will be over. He'll be able to stop sweating it and we can have fun.

"Hi, honey," Mom pulls me from Adrian and squishes me in a hug. "I'm so glad you made it."

"Mom," I pry myself from her death grip. "I was here a few hours ago helping you set up, stop acting like I've been tucked away on some deserted island. Adrian doesn't need to see all the weirdness on the first night."

"Excuse me for being happy to see you," she harrumphs. Now that I'm free, she pulls Adrian into one of her tighter than necessary hugs. His arms are squished against his sides, and his shoulders are so tense they almost touch his ears. It's pretty funny, but I'll never let him see the smile playing at my lips. "You must be Adrian. It's so nice to meet you. Sophia hasn't stopped talking about you."

"Mom." My voice is shrill. No longer smiling, I bury

my face in my hands. This is mortifying. Peeking between my fingers, I see Jay doing his best to hold in his laughter. Asshole. I guess he's not worried about the least party-like music playing anymore. "Would you please stop embarrassing me?"

"Oh, sweetie," she releases Adrian and snickers, "that's my job as a parent. It's written in the top spot in every parenting guide."

"I'm Lisa, by the way." She pats Adrian on the arm, and from his small step back, I can tell he's trying to avoid another hug.

"Now that my mom has forced herself on you," I flash a frown toward Mom. She isn't phased in the least. Maybe it really is part of her job to embarrass the hell out of me. "This is my dad, Tom."

"Nice to meet you, son." Dad holds out his hand, and Adrian quickly offers his own. After two shakes, Adrian's hand is back in mine. "Feel free to ignore my wife. She has a flare for the dramatic."

"At least I still know how to have fun," she mutters under her breath. At least I know where Jay gets his weird attitude from.

If he's like Mom, I'm much more like my dad. Only not quite as reserved. I wouldn't be able to work at the shop if I never talked to anyone. What can I say? Dad is the yin to Mom's yang. They make sense in an odd sort of way. I wonder if people think that about me and Adrian. Hell, the girls at the shop still haven't said anything, though they definitely suspect something.

Dad studies Adrian, taking him in from head to toe. Adrian's palm is sweating in my hand, and he's rocking back and forth, clearly uncomfortable. The urge to wipe my hand on my dress is strong, but I push it aside. Adrian doesn't need me pulling away from him while he's under my dad's scrutiny.

He points to Adrian's forearm, "That's some fine ink you have there. Did you design it?"

"Yes, sir," Adrian's voice cracks. "I design all of my tattoos to keep from being dissatisfied with the outcome. Bianca, Charleigh, and Corey have all done the artwork in the end."

"You have talent," Dad nods his head. "Have you ever tattooed Sophia?"

My boyfriend chuckles. This is territory he knows well, and I'm thankful to my dad for bringing up a subject he knew would calm Adrian down. "No, she hasn't let me... yet. The time will come, though." He gives me a sexy smirk. I want to drag him to my childhood room and let him show me where exactly he wants to put the ink. "Honestly, I think she's scared. She didn't actually talk to me until last week, and that's only because I ordered supplies I didn't need."

"Hey," my hand makes a thwack sound as it makes contact with his chest, "you weren't exactly welcoming either."

Dad smiles at our playful banter. "Can I steal my daughter from you for a moment?"

"There's no need to steal her, she was yours first."

That puddle on the ground is totally me. He makes my heart melt and beat faster all at the same time.

Standing on my tiptoes, I press a quick peck to his cheek, and he heads toward Jay. The only person at this party that he really knows. At least they are getting along now. Once he's out of earshot, I turn toward my dad. "What do you think of him? And be honest." I don't need them suppressing their thoughts this time around.

"I like him," Dad smiles. "He seems like a good guy from what I can tell, and he's been making sure you're safe. That's what matters the most to me."

"Dad," I roll my eyes. "I don't need someone to take care of me. My life isn't some fifties sitcom."

"You think I don't know that you're capable of taking care of yourself," he places his hands on my shoulders and waits until I give him my full attention. It's hard because I want to know what my brother and boyfriend are laughing about. Please don't let Jay be telling him any horrid childhood stories. Focus, Soph. My eyes land on my father. "You left a shitty relationship even though you were terrified. That takes guts, sweetheart. I like Adrian's protectiveness. He hasn't stopped looking at you since he joined your brother."

I want to look back toward them, but don't. Instead, I keep my eyes focused on Dad. "He makes me happy, and I feel safe with him. Not like he's my protector," I wave away my father's concern. "He feels like home. The person I can rely on."

"Just make sure you aren't moving too fast, Sophia,"

Dad pulls me in for a hug. "I know you feel the connection, and it's possible that he's it for you, like your mom was for me. I don't want to see you hurting again."

"I know, daddy," I squeeze him. "The emotions I feel with him are real, though. He lifts me up, unlike Dawson who would constantly put me down. He's the real deal."

"As long as you're sure," he releases me. "Now, go have fun. Your brother is only here for a couple more days."

Without another word I walk, well jog would be the more appropriate term, toward the man that I can see a future with. Who gives a damn if people think it's too soon. My heart knows what it wants, and it wants him.

adrian

THIS IS a night for the history books. I never thought I'd be having fun hanging out with Sophia's family. Tom has been asking about my tattoos all night, and Lisa has fretted over me and her kids for the last hour. Our hands have been filled with either drinks or food, and I'm going to have to start working out if she keeps feeding me.

"Are you ready to go?" Sophia jumps on my back. Her sundress flies up with the movement. I scoot back until the backs of our legs hit the table, and she's seated on it. I can't have Jay's friends attempting to catch a peek at what is underneath. I'd be shocked if they didn't grow up with crushes on her throughout their friendship with Jay. I know I would have.

"Yep," I spin until we're face to face. "I just need to grab my phone charger and tell Tom and Lisa goodbye."

She pats my chest, "And you were worried tonight would be a disaster." She leans back until she holds all of her weight on her elbows. "I think they may actually like you better than they do me."

"Did you want me to hold in my awesome?" I tower over her, noses almost touching. "Just know that nobody likes you as much as I do right this minute."

I know the exact moment she feels my growing erection against her. Her squeal is loud and piercing. Jay throws his hands over his ears and glares at us in disgust. "You realize people eat there, right? Please don't do anything on that table. I'm begging you." He almost slides to his knees to beg.

Sophia opens her mouth to torture her baby brother, but her lips are met by my finger. "Shhhh. Leave him be. He's not going back to your place with us is he?"

Eyes wide, guessing at what my plans might include, she shakes her head. "No, he's crashing here until he goes back to school on Sunday. I just have to meet them for breakfast that morning before he goes."

"Do you want to go to your place or mine?" Her apartment feels homier than mine, but I want her in *my* bed.

Her mouth forms a tiny "oh". From shock or excitement, I have no clue. But... I can't wait to find out. She jumps up and knocks me back. Her hand is in mine before I've had a chance to find my feet, and I'm whirled around toward the side gate. "Wait, Sophia. I still have to tell your parents goodbye."

"Really?" She waves her hand from her head to her feet. "Because most guys wouldn't be thinking about their girlfriend's parents as they're being dragged to the car."

She has a point, and she is clearly the one in charge. I'll follow her wherever she leads me. "I guess I'm inviting myself to breakfast on Sunday. Do you have a phone charger I can use until then?"

A cord appears out of nowhere from her purse. "I've got you covered," she shoves it back in the tiny bag without issue.

I could dwell on the magic that is a woman's purse for hours. How they fit so many things in such a small area. Sophia is pulling me along behind her, and I follow her like a puppy on a leash, not truly knowing how this night is going to end. If I'm lucky, it will be wrapped around her.

* * *

We are rushing up the stairs to my apartment. We're tripping over each other's feet, racing to see who can get there first. Of course, it will be me because she's never been here. She doesn't know which floor I'm on, or the door that leads to my not so humble abode, and I have the key. Her fingers are clasped in mine when we reach my apartment. Warm kisses pepper my cheek, my neck, any available surface she can reach. The keys slip from my shaking hand before I can put it in the keyhole. Sophia puts me on edge, in a good way, and I don't know if I possess the control to take my time once we're behind closed doors. "If you keep doing that, it's only going to take longer until we are inside. "

"You mean, until you're inside," she's giggling. Happiness looks good on her, and I hope I can be the one that continues to put that smile on her face. Ridiculous innuendos or not.

"How much have you had to drink?" I don't want to offend her, but she's not normally this free with her words. Innocent flirting is more her style. This...while nice is something altogether new.

She bends down to grab the keys at the same time I do. Pain shoots from the top of my head, and she's rubbing hers. "Would you believe me if I said none?"

"Probably not." It's just not possible. Even when we went out for drinks last week she held on to her propriety. Her head was still on straight even after two beers. Alcohol *was* flowing freely at the going away party. Jay, and his friends, were sneaking it every chance they could. Tom and Lisa knew, though. It's why all his friends had to stay at their house. They didn't want to be responsible for anything that might happen afterward.

"Then you," she taps my nose with her pointer finger, as if I'm a small child that needs adoration. "Would be correct."

I put the key in the door knob, but I don't turn it. Not yet. "Are you sure you want to do this tonight? We can always go back to the car and I drive you home."

She winces at my question, lip quivering. "Do you not want me?" Shit she's going to cry. I've never seen her truly tipsy and I have a sneaking suspicion she's an emotional drunk. It's time to see just how far the emotion pendulum swings.

I pull my hand away from the door knob, key still sticking out from it, and frame Sophia's face with both of my hands. "Of course, I want you. I have wanted you for a lot longer than you think. Before I even knew that I might want to date you." Her skin is soft as I stroke it with my thumb, doing what I can to ease her fears.

Worry is hidden within her eyes, warring with the words that came out of my mouth. I hate that prick for making her think she's not enough. That she's not beautiful. I will do everything I can to make sure she knows how much I adore her.

"Let's go inside." She turns the key, the sharp click of the lock releasing thunderous in this silent hallway. Pushing the door open wider, she walks in before me. Anticipation roars through my body. Not only for what might come to fruition tonight, but also for what it could mean for our future.

I'm not sure what Sophia expected my house to look like, but this definitely isn't it. She's squinting her eyes and tapping her fingers against her leg. "Wow." She looks at me then back at the living room. "It's very... clean and sleek."

Well, that's one way to put it. "I'm rarely ever home since I'm always at the shop. And, I like to think of it as modern."

She nods her head. I have a feeling she's placating me

because she doesn't want to hurt my feelings. "It is. It just doesn't seem like you. Don't get me wrong," she waves her hands in the air trying to take the words back. "I like it. But I envisioned your space being more masculine and homey."

Now would probably be a bad time to tell her that the modern decoration didn't happen until after I met Miranda for the first time. It was my way of trying to impress her, and it failed miserably. She hated it almost as much as Sophia seems to hate it. Letting the comment hang, I gently shut the door behind us and lock it. "Do you want anything to drink, or a snack or something?"

Why would I offer her a snack? I never buy them. Ninety percent of my food is from restaurants and the only thing I keep stocked in my pantry is Ramen noodles, cereal, and milk. If I didn't need the milk for the cereal, I probably wouldn't have that either. She gives me a small smile, and shakes her head. "No, I'm good. The location of a bathroom would be great, though."

"Oh, sure." Now the question is do I send her to the guest bathroom in the hallway or the one in my room. I've been out of the game for so long, I have no idea what to do, or which is more acceptable. "There's one in the hallway to the right, or you can use the one in my room all the way at the end of the hall."

"Thanks. I'll, uh, be right back." She rushes down the hallway.

Instead of watching to see which one she picks, and secretly hoping it's the one in my room since I don't know if the guest bathroom has anything in it, I go to the kitchen and grab a glass out of the cabinet. My throat is suddenly as dry as a desert. Each swallow like sandpaper. The beer in my refrigerator is calling my name, inviting me to take a sip and loosen my nerves. I don't want to do that, though. If there is any chance, I get to be wrapped up with Sophia tonight, I want to have a clear head so I can remember every single detail.

It's been well over five minutes since Sophia excused herself. My first reaction is that something is wrong. Maybe she passed out? Then fear grabs hold of me. Or, maybe she's crawled out of the window to the fire escape to avoid being anywhere near me. That would be my luck. I finally find a girl I'm head over heels for, and she bails.

"Sophia," I call out. She doesn't answer. Maybe she really did do something that drastic to bail. I should have just taken her home, or left her at her parents' house. Fuck, I'm in way over my head.

My steps are steady as I walk to the bathroom in the hallway. The door is wide open but there is no Sophia. There is only one option left. My bedroom door is mere feet from the bathroom, but it feels like ages as I cross the hardwood floor to the entrance. The door is closed even though I'm sure I left it open.

My hand is on the knob, and I'm terrified of what may be awaiting me on the other side if she passed out. Turning the knob, I swing the door open, and almost fall back in shock.

Sophia is in here alright, but she isn't asleep, hurt, or sick. She's lying on my bed and my pillows are stacked behind her. A temporary throne for the queen that's taking over every rational thought I have. The only items on her body... a black lace bra and panty set. My jaw hits the floor. If this is a dream, nobody better wake me up.

"It took you long enough," she grins devilishly, "I thought I was going to have to give up and go to sleep."

"You pl-planned this?" She will never cease to amaze me.

"Yep." She crooks her finger and motions for me to come closer. "Are you going to stand there all night? Or are you going to come lie down with me."

I've officially died and gone to heaven. What did I do to deserve this woman? My karma must be good. That's the only explanation for the sight before me. My feet listen before my brain, and I'm across the room in seconds. My shirt hits the floor, and I climb on the bed next to her. "Is there anything in particular you have in mind?"

"Lean back and I'll show you," the words are a promise, and I can't wait to see what she has in store for me.

sophia

HOLY SHIT. I'm completely out of my element here. It's a good thing I had a few more drinks than normal at the party. Other-wise... I wouldn't have the courage to be as forward as I am.

It took him so long to come back here, I thought he'd forgotten about me. Now he's lying next to me and I'm not sure what to do. Showing him how much I want him should be easy, but it's not. I haven't been with anyone since Dawson. Swearing off guys will do that to a gal. I need him to know, though.

"Are you surprised?" My voice is high and squeaky. Not exactly the tone I'm going for. It's definitely less seductive and more scared out of my mind.

He nods, unable to say anything, or maybe he doesn't trust his voice. His throat bobs as he swallows. "Very," his scratchy voice meets my ears, and I melt. At least I know he's as nervous as I am.

Leaning over him, I press a kiss to his cheek. The stubble tickles my lips and I'm shocked to find I actually like it. Dawson was always clean-shaven. Even when we'd have sex at night, he would go "clean up" before he came to bed. It was weird. No weirder than him popping into my thoughts as I'm trying to seduce my boyfriend.

Shoving those thoughts away, I kiss Adrian's neck. His breaths come out faster, and his heart is racing beneath my palm. His reaction turns me on more than I thought possible. My lips trail down his body. Collarbone, chest, and these lickable abs are the only things I focus on. Who in the hell has muscles like this on their stomach? I feel flabby compared to him, but he doesn't seem to mind. Looking up at him, his eyes are trained on me. Nothing else matters to him, only me.

"Do you know how beautiful you are?" His voice is a whisper in the quiet room. He pulls me up until I'm face to face with him. I shake my head and try to look away, but he doesn't let me. He cups my face and presses his mouth to mine. "You are stunning, and I am going to show you just how much."

* * *

I never want to leave this bed. Well, maybe for my own bed. Adrian's apartment is nice, but it doesn't feel like home. There's a part of him missing from this space. I can't put my finger on why. It's just a feeling I have. He lost a part of himself somewhere and I hope he finds it again.

He's in the bathroom, cleaning up after making love to me. I can't help but notice the difference between him and Dawson. Adrian took his time, bringing me close to the edge and pulling back. Teasing me and constantly making sure that I was okay. Never letting himself be the focus, it was always on me. Dawson on the other hand hardly made sex enjoyable for me. He'd do whatever it took to get off, and not worry about me. Those times alone should have showed me how selfish he is, and how little he cares about me. Instead of seeing the truth behind all the pretty words, I let him continue to use me like his own personal play thing.

A phone pings and I sit up to rummage through my pile of clothes on the floor. I know that stupid thing is over here somewhere. Though, I could have sworn I put it on silent. I didn't want tonight to be interrupted by anything. I finally find it in the pocket of my dress. The screen is black and there aren't any indications that a message came through. It must have been Adrian's but who would be texting him this late at night? The only people I've ever seen him talk to are the girls at the shop. I know they are busy with their own boyfriends, and it can't be them.

Part of me wants to see who is texting him. It would be a huge invasion of privacy, though. If I start obsessing over who he's talking to, I'm no better than Dawson, and he's the last person I want to be like. When another text notification comes through, curiosity gets the best of me.

I have one foot on the floor, and I'm searching through the piles of blankets on the bed for a shirt to put on when the bathroom door creaks open. Adrian must see something in my expression when he looks at me. "Is something wrong?"

Panic over almost being caught doing something I shouldn't be doing grips me. My palms are slightly shaking and my heart is beating so hard, and loud, I'm sure he can hear it on the other side of the room. "No, I was just looking for something to put on. I'm cold."

He rummages through a drawer, and pulls out a clean shirt. "Are you sure?" He walks to the bed, and sits down beside me.

"Yeah," my voice wobbles.

"Lift up your arms," Adrian unfolds the shirt in his hands and slips it over my arms, then my head, before pulling it over my exposed body. "Was this," he waves at the crumpled blanket on the bed, "too soon?"

God, here he is being so kind and considerate. Making sure that I'm okay when I was seconds away from betraying his trust. "No, not at all. I'm pretty sure I'm the one who instigated it." I force a smile onto my face. He doesn't realize that it's not a real one, though.

"Good, because I don't regret one minute of it. Being with you is like finding my way home again."

"Why do you say that?" The apartment is silent, except for the air conditioner turning on.

He grabs my hand, turning it until my palm is facing up, and places a gentle kiss in the center. "I was lost for a long time after leaving Miranda. I questioned my perception of the things that happened, and realized that I was only a commodity to her. A phase she was going through before meeting her ideal person."

This is my opening to find out why he never told me he was engaged before. "So, I guess things were pretty serious with her?"

He laughs, but there's no amusement behind the sound. It's bitter and full of self-loathing. "Yeah, you could say that. At least, they were for me." He takes a deep breath, readying himself for whatever he is about to say. "She approached me at a bar, and I gravitated toward her immediately. We began dating and I changed my entire lifestyle to suit her."

"But you were still tattooing, right?" I can't imagine him ever giving up the one thing he loves for somebody else. It's something I would never ask anybody after having it demanded from me. Losing yourself to what you think is love is like dying a slow and painful death.

"No, I never gave up my job. But I changed my apartment, what I wore, and my focus. It all became about her, and after a year of dating I proposed to her." He's staring at me, but not really seeing me. Focusing on getting everything off his mind. He's doing what needs to be done in order to protect himself from whatever I might say. "Things were fine, at least I thought they were. After being together for another year, without any mention of a wedding date, she began pulling away. Always starting fights with me because of my hours at the shop, working late, and being just downright bitchy. Charleigh and Bianca saw the shift in me and were not happy about it. If it wasn't for them, I might have given up everything for her."

"I'm sorry she tried to change you." It's a feeling I know all too well. Being told you aren't good enough, or that what you're doing isn't acceptable. It's no way to go through life. It's no way to live your life. Forcing yourself to be someone else's ideal partner. It makes life boring and shuts everyone else out.

"It's my fault. She never came out and asked me to be any different than what I am, but I did it anyway out of fear of losing her. It's why I was so reluctant to form any sort of relationship with you when you started working at the shop. My strong attraction to you was similar to what I felt when I met her, and I didn't want to give myself up again. But you were different. Someone I could see a possibility with."

It's completely understandable because I was leery of him as well. The instant attraction and butterflies in my stomach, along with the intrigue of Adrian, forced me to long for him from afar. And now that Dawson could potentially be creeping in the shadows of my life, it's probably the worst time to consider a relationship. "I get it. It was the same with Dawson. I lost myself to him with each demand he made. I was stupid for pushing away my family and friends because that's what he wanted. I allowed this person to drag me down to the pits of hell within my own mind, and it took me a long time to recover. I'm glad you told me about her though. When you mentioned her in the car, I was worried that you might still have some sort of feelings for her."

"Not in the slightest," he laughs, "she's history and has been for a while." He moves the comforter around, making room for us to lie down. "Do you want to stay the night?"

"It's almost morning," I point to the clock he has on his nightstand. It's weird seeing one there because most people rely on their phones to wake them up. "But... there's no other place I'd rather be."

He pulls me down, and within seconds my back is to his chest, feeling the steady rhythm of his breathing. A wave of peace flows over me. This is exactly where I'm meant to be. It may be fast, and I really don't care. Love doesn't follow a timeline. It finds you when you least expect it, and throws your whole world off balance.

I snuggle deeper into his embrace. "Oh, someone sent you a text message while you were in the bathroom. I thought it was my phone but I didn't have any notifications." I hold my breath, waiting to see what his response will be.

"That can wait," he strengthens his hold on me, securing me to him, "all that matters right now is you, right here, in my arms. The world could be burning around us, and I wouldn't give a damn."

Rather than argue with him, I bask in the feel of him against me. Knowing without a doubt that he'll still be holding me against him in the morning. Accepting his drink offer last week was the best decision I've made in a very long time.

adrian

THE SHRILL RINGING of my phone startles me awake. I almost knock Sophia off the bed in my rush to answer it. There's only one person who actually takes the time to call someone. "What is that noise?" Sophia groans into the pillow. "Make it stop."

I kiss her forehead and whisper, "It's my phone. Give me just a second."

The ringing stops and starts again before I'm to the dresser. My fingers are around it and pressing the answer icon before the ringing ends again. "Hello," I'm breathless after rushing across the room.

"Finally," Corey's voice booms through the speaker. "Did you not get my texts last night?"

Damn it, Sophia told me she heard my phone go off, but I was too wrapped up in her to check it. I don't regret it one bit. Telling her about my shortcomings with Miranda felt good. We both know exactly where we stand with each other. There are no secrets, no ulterior motives, and that is exactly how things are supposed to be when you start a relationship with someone.

Corey is calling my name through the phone and I remember I never answered him, too busy replaying everything that happened last night. The feel of her skin as I dragged my fingers down her body. The sounds she made when I took her over the edge again and again. I could spend hours exploring every inch of her beautiful body. I shake my head. Now is not the time with my boss on the phone. "Sorry, I was preoccupied last night."

"I'm sure you were," he chuckles softly. "Anyway, I need you at the shop early. Marshall called me last night, and Bianca is sick. She's running a fever and throwing up. The whole nine yards."

"That's something I could have gone without knowing, Corey." Nobody wants to hear about someone else puking their guts up. We're like family at the shop, but even that is a little too much information.

"Sorry," he says, though he doesn't sound sorry at all. I swear his life goal is to make me uncomfortable. "Anyway, like I said, I need you at the shop as soon as you can get here. I'm heading in right now to help where I can, and take on some of her clients for the day."

"I'll get ready now, and head that way." Ugh, I'm not supposed to go in for another two hours. I planned on using that time to wake Sophia up in the best way possible, or at least help keep her from being so grumpy this morning.

"If you could, bring Soph with you. We'll need her help calling Bianca's appointments for the next few days. I'm not sure how long she'll be out, but it's better to reschedule what we can now, just in case."

"You got it. I'll see you in a bit." Groaning, I end the call and set the phone back on the dresser.

"I have to get up, don't I?" Sophia's voice from under the blanket scares me and I hit my toe on the bottom of the dresser.

Attempting to keep the pain out of my voice because holy shit does this hurt, I stumble back to the bed. "Unfortunately." I pull the blanket back, revealing Sophia's face and bed hair one slow inch at a time. My breath stops as I take her in. She's beautiful when she first wakes up, when she's dressed up and ready for a party, or when she has her hair pulled back with a headband while at work. I want nothing more than to stay cuddled up with her in bed all day. Naked or clothed, I don't care. I only want her. But we have a job that needs us as soon as possible, and I hit pause on my daydreaming. One day we will be able to have that, but for now… duty calls. "Corey needs us to come in, Bianca is sick."

"So much for getting my beauty sleep," she sits up, almost hitting me in the head. "Can we run by my place? I don't want to wear the same clothes as last night."

"Sure thing." I stand up, pulling her out of the bed and onto her feet. I open the drawer where I keep my sweats and pull a pair out. Handing them to her, I say, "Put these on. I'll get a bag together and I'll just shower at your house so we don't take too much time. Corey sounded like he was in a panic."

She rolls her eyes as she slips my pants on. "Corey always panics when things don't go according to plan. I'm sure it's not that big of a deal." Seeing her in my clothes turns me on. She looks hot as hell with my rumpled shirt covering her body, and my pants almost too big to stay up on their own. Despite her eye makeup being a little smeared, which I'm not going to mention because she'll freak out, she is stunning.

"Probably not," I sigh. "But he's getting older, as much as he doesn't like to admit it, and I don't want him worrying himself to the point of sickness."

"You have a point," she grabs her clothes off the floor and folds them in a neat pile. "Are you ready?"

"Yep," I grab her and we walk out of my apartment. Sharing my space with her was a good decision even if the person my apartment used to represent is no longer here.

Thirty minutes later we are in Sophia's apartment, and it feels great to be back here after staying at my place last night. Not that it was bad or anything when we were there. The only thing that made it feel more alive is Sophia. She made me *want* to be home for once. I guess if I get right down to it, I want to be where she is.

My lovely girlfriend is running around the apartment like a lunatic turning baskets over, trying to find clean towels and clothes. "You know we can make this process easier by taking a shower together," I wink at her.

"Nope," she shakes her head, throwing two towels into the air in victory. "That would definitely take longer, and you said we have to be there as soon as we can." She shoves one of the towels into my chest. "We wouldn't want to disappoint the boss, now would we?" With a quick peck on the cheek, she turns toward her room. "You can use the guest bath. I'm sure Jay's crap is still in there."

Would she be mad if I waited a few moments and jumped in the shower anyway? My steps are silent as I make my way to her room, and bathroom. Seconds away from reaching the door, I hear the lock click. Damn it, she must have figured out my plan. Guess I'm taking a shower in here, then. Most likely a cold one.

"Corey is going to be pissed we're here later than anticipated," Sophia groans as we get out of the car. I can make it to the shop within fifteen minutes from my place. But she lives further out than I do, and traffic is a bitch.

"He'll be fine," I take her hand in mine. "He's lucky I even answered the phone. I had other plans for us this morning."

"Oh, you did?" One of her eyebrows rises. "And what exactly were they?"

"You'll never find out," I grin. "Let's get in there before he has a heart attack or something. I imagine Charleigh isn't much help, if she's even here yet. She hates mornings more than you do. And if Jake ate her cereal again, she'll be in a worse mood."

She looks across the street, eyeing the restaurant. "I completely forgot to eat this morning. It's going to be a long freaking day."

She's not wrong. Today is going to be brutal. Getting sick on the weekend isn't an ideal situation. Some of the younger crowd will be coming in to get those last-minute tattoos before heading off to school. Memories of their summer vacations, friendships formed and hearts broken. As horrible as it sounds, those of my favorite ones to do because they mean something to the person getting them. "Most likely, but we've got this."

"You're finally here," Corey's voice booms through the shop as soon my foot is through the front door. "This is what y'all call quick?"

"I'm so sorry, Corey," Sophia immediately apologizes, hand trying to slip from mine. I grasp it tighter. I'm not letting her hide our relationship from everyone, even though they suspect it already. "We had to go by my house so I could shower and change. It takes forever to get here from there sometimes." She winces when she realizes she said "we." The cat's out of the bag now.

Corey walks around the front desk and gives Sophia a

side hug. "It's okay. I was trying to figure out how to read your scheduling system so I could start calling Bianca's clients. Would you get a list together and split it up so we're all calling the same amount of people?"

"Sure thing," she nods. This time she successfully pulls her hand out of mine because Corey holds me back when I try to follow her.

"You aren't going to break this girl's heart, are you?" He whispers so that Sophia can't hear him. "I love you like family, but if you screw things up with her, and she quits... I'm making you sit up here at the desk."

"No, I'm not going to break her heart," I roll my eyes. "I care about her. More than I thought capable after a short amount of time. But she might be it for me."

"I never thought I'd see the day after all the bullshit with Miranda," he grins. "At least Soph fits in with your life. She knows the lifestyle, the hours, and she loves ink as much as the rest of us."

I clap him on the back, nodding in agreement. "I'm glad I have your approval. I met her parents last night, and I think it went well."

"That's good." He points to my area. "Now, go get your shit set up so you can help us make calls."

"Hey, Corey," Sophia calls. "Before you head back to the office, do I split it into groups of three or make a list for Charleigh, too. I didn't see her light on when we came in."

"Make a list for Charleigh, too. She'll be here soon." He's resigned, knowing that soon could mean in a hour or two. She better get here soon since we have to make all these calls before getting ready for our own appointments. I wonder if she knows we might have to ink some of Bianca's clients, too.

Twenty-five minutes later, Charleigh makes her appearance, and if the scowl on her face is any indication, she's not in a good mood. "If that motherfucker doesn't stop eating *my* cereal, I'm going to smother him in his sleep."

"Trouble in paradise?" I laugh. "I thought the family life was suiting you well."

"It'd be a hell of a lot better if he'd stop eating the last of my cereal, pick up more when he does, or at least tell me we are out." She stomps to the front desk. "But, no. He doesn't do any of that. Instead, my day is ruined because when I go to pour myself a bowl, only crumbs are left."

"You sound like an old married couple," Sophia snorts. "I can already see the fallout. 'Relationship gone sour over cereal. Fellows, keep your pantry stocked.'"

"That's not funny," Charleigh pouts. "Okay, maybe it is. But now is not the time for jokes."

"I'll make your day better, then," Sophia hands her the list of people she needs to call. "Everyone on here needs to be called and rescheduled, or moved into your schedule."

"When I'm hangry isn't the best time for me to be calling people, but I better or Corey will be all over my ass." She squeezes the list in her fist and walks to her room.

"I'll be right back," I call out to Sophia before walking out the front door. The girls are hungry and they both hate mornings. The least I can do is run across the street and grab some food. I believe I should win employee of the month after this. I'm saving people everywhere from their horrible morning moods.

sophia

"SO," Adrian leans against the counter. "What are we doing tonight?"

"I don't know what you're doing, but I'll be going to Asheville." Grinning, I take the blank forms from the counter and put them in the basket underneath. Closing time is probably my favorite since Adrian and I started dating. We don't have a ton of free nights with the shop being open late, but we make the most of it. Usually, we hang out at each other's apartments and watch movies. By the time we are done working for the night, we don't really want to be around other people.

"Why are you going to Asheville?" He scrunches his nose. "There's literally nothing in that tiny town."

Rolling my eyes, I shake my head and sigh, "I already told you this."

"No, you didn't," he argues. "I would have remembered."

"Then you would know that tonight is the book club Charleigh and Bianca invited me to," I sing song. It annoys him when I do that, but deep down he most likely thinks it's cute.

"Wait," he sputters. "Charleigh reads?"

"Why is that so hard to believe?" Charleigh walks into the lobby. "I do occasionally pick up a book."

Adrian shrugs and comes around the counter, both of his arms wrap around my waist. "I've just never seen you with a book. This one," he squeezes me, "however, constantly has her Kindle in her hands. I have to pry it away just to watch a movie with her."

"What can I say?" I spin around and throw my arms around his neck. "The scenes I imagine from the books I read are better than the ones on the TV screen."

"If you say so," he mutters. "I've hardly seen you since you stopped letting me stay over all the time."

It's true. I've been trying to force some sort of space between us, even if I want to be with him all the time. I don't want to lose myself to another relationship. Besides, I don't think Dawson is following me. Those creepy being watched vibes haven't resurfaced in quite a while. "You'll survive," my lips graze his with a quick peck. "We have all day Monday to do whatever we want."

"Does that mean we don't have to leave the bed?"

"If that's how you choose to spend it." My grin is mischievous and he lifts me up on the counter.

"Ugh, gross." Charleigh groans. "Get a room. Or go somewhere I don't have to witness it."

"Dude," Adrian says over my shoulder. "You and Jake are the exact same way. You shouldn't throw stones."

"Whatever," she throws her purse over her shoulder. "I'll see you at the coffee shop, Soph." She eyes Adrian, not trusting that I'll show up. "Do you need the address?"

"Nope," I say. "I already have it programmed in my phone. I'll be behind you in just a few."

Waving, she walks out of the shop, and Adrian pulls me to the edge of the counter. "Finally, the grouchy one is gone. I can have my way with you before you have to go."

"We don't have time for that, Adrian," I giggle as he presses warm, wet kisses to my neck. "If I don't show up, Charleigh is likely to come back here and kick your ass."

"I'm not scared of her," he laughs. "For real, though. I miss waking up to you in the mornings. Are you sure *he's* not following you? I have no problem waiting for you at your apartment to make sure everything goes okay."

"I'm sure," I place my hand against his chest. His heart beat is steady and strong. The constant I didn't know I needed in my life. "But if I feel that way again, you'll be the first to know." Leaning my head on his shoulder, I let out a breath. "Honestly, I'm beginning to think I imagined it all and my brain was playing tricks on me. It's been almost two months and I haven't felt watched. There's nothing to worry about."

"If you say so," he relents, knowing he's fighting a losing battle. "I suppose I'll let you leave now, as much as it pains me to watch you go."

"You act like you won't see me for days," I snort. "You have clearly been hanging out with my mom way too much."

"What can I say? She loves me," he presses a kiss to my forehead and helps me off the counter.

"Not as much as I do," I mumble.

"What?" He puts his hands on the counter, caging me in. "Did you say what I think you did?"

Shit, he heard that? I need to get better at keeping my thoughts inside my brain. "Maybe," I hedge, ducking under his arm. I run around to the front of the counter, putting it between us.

"Oh no," he follows me around. "You don't get to say something like that and then leave. Do you? Love me, that is."

It's the moment of truth. "Yes," I say on a sigh. And I do. I feel more deeply for him in the two and a half months we've been together than I ever did in the two years I was with Dawson. He's my home even when he's staying at his place. He's the first, and last, person I talk to every single day. It may be quick to some people, especially since most of our time is spent within the walls of Life in Ink, but who gives a shit what other people think. My family loves him, and I do too.

"I love you too, Sophia," he pulls me into his arms

and seals his lips to mine. It's a good thing we are the only ones here and the shop is mostly dark. This kiss is one for the record books. There's no tongue, but it's probably the most passionate kiss I've ever received. This man has seared himself into my soul, and I don't ever want to lose him. He pulls away before things get carried away. "And, I'm not just saying that. You are my person, and I'm not letting you go."

If I had a quarter for every time Adrian has made me swoon, I'd be rich. My heart is racing and I fear it may beat right out of my chest. Catching my breath, I lean against his chest. "I should probably go before the girls freak out. I'll text you when I leave. Maybe you can come over?"

"Yes," he pumps his fist in the air and jumps up and down. "I get to wake up to your beautiful grumpy self in the morning."

"You are such a dork," I laugh. Standing on tiptoes, I kiss him on the cheek. "I'll see you in a few hours."

"Be careful," he stares down at me. "If you're too tired to drive, call me and I'll pick you up."

"Will do." I walk toward the door. When I look over my shoulder, he's still watching me. Gah, the attention he gives me is more than I could ask for. With him, I know I'm enough. I don't have to pretend to be anything else.

* * *

This coffee shop is as clever as its name. Brews Clue's is cute and small, but not too small. There's still plenty of room to move around without bumping into anyone. We're the only people still here, and I can feel the employees stare at us, willing us to get up so they can close the store.

Amelia, Bianca, and I are the only people who actually read the book. It looks like Adrian was correct earlier. It's not that Charleigh doesn't like to read; she just doesn't have the time. Any free time she has is consumed by Jake and Layla when they have her for the weekend. It's a shame they didn't read it because it was hysterical and steamy. *How to Date a Douchebag* is definitely one of my favorite reads this year.

"So, Sophie," Bianca sits up in her chair. "How are things going with you and Adrian?"

Charleigh laughs, louder than what I think is warranted. "How do you think it's going?" She crosses her arms. "I swear, every time I go to the break room they are making out and acting like two teenagers that can't control themselves."

"I'm not even going to broach that one," Bianca smirks at Charleigh. "I seem to remember someone being lovestruck when they first started dating."

Tonya, Jake's ex and the mother of his child, laughs. "I think there is something about new relationships that make us completely lose our shit and not care how we act."

Amelia groans. "You and Reaf still act like that, so I don't know what you mean by 'new' relationships."

Tonya throws a piece of her muffin at her cousin, and Amelia ducks.

This is getting out of control. "Things are going great with Adrian. I may have let the three-word sentence slip today." My cheeks are warm, and I'm certain I'm blushing. I'm not embarrassed by it. I never thought I would feel that way about a guy. The way of an old spinster was the direction I was set on heading toward. Even though I liked Adrian for far longer than I want to admit, I didn't think he'd ever show an interest in me.

"What did he say?" Charleigh leans forward, eager to hear what happened.

"You know exactly what he said," Bianca laughs. "He's been gaga over her for a long time. I think he fell in love with her before they even started dating."

I'm not sure about that, but I know I was definitely in lust with him before that night we had drinks. It was a little pathetic how much I paid attention to him when I thought he wasn't looking. It definitely felt like those days when you're in high school and you like someone and aren't sure how to approach them. Luckily for me, he came to me before I could gather up the courage to seek him out.

My phone dings with a message.

Adrian: Are you ever going to head back? I want to show you just how much I love you. ;)

Rolling my eyes, I glance up at the girls. They all know what's coming. Charleigh is the first to speak up. "Get out of here, and cuddle up with your boyfriend. We all know that's who is texting you."

"Are you sure?" I feel horrible for running out on them.

"Yep," Tonya answers. "They are about to kick us out anyway. Go hang out with your man."

"Thanks," I grab my book, and put in my bag. "Let me know the date for next month. And the book we're reading." I make eye contact with each and every one of them. "This time actually read the book. Who knows... you could learn some things, if you know what I mean." I wink at them and walk out of the coffee shop.

Sophia: I'm leaving now. I should be home in forty-five minutes.

Adrian: Yes! I'll be there in an hour.

The hair on the back of my neck rises, and that feeling I haven't had in a while is back in full force. Brushing it off, I rush to my car, get in and lock the doors. Nothing is going to keep me from Adrian right now. Even a pesky feeling that is most likely nothing.

* * *

Music blares through my radio. Taylor Swift is the soundtrack for my drive home. The car is the only place I listen to her to keep from being ridiculed. Jay is always telling me there is better music out there, and maybe there is. But there's nothing wrong with listening to what makes your heart happy. And *this* is what makes my heart fill up with joy. Other music does too, but it's a Swift sort of night.

The apartment complex is quiet when I park my car. Adrian's car, nor his motorcycle, are anywhere in sight. I figured he would be here before I was. Hell, I wouldn't have been surprised if he was hanging out here until I got home. Before, that would have completely freaked me out. Now... I'm happy to be with somebody who is genuinely excited to see me and wants to be around me without controlling my every move.

Grabbing my phone from the cup holder, I throw it in my bag and open the car door. Maybe I can surprise him with nothing but a robe when he gets here. It's definitely something he would appreciate. Hopefully, I still have the rope from when I was in college. It's nothing fancy or anything like that, but I think it would get the point across. My bed is one of my favorite places to spend time with him. Even if we're only cuddling and watching movies. Saying the "L" word is a big deal. I want to do something memorable.

One of these days, I'm going to try my hardest to get a ground floor apartment. Walking up these stairs after I have been on my feet all day is getting old. Especially, when I decide to wear boots with wedges instead of a pair of tennis shoes. Not my brightest idea, but I wasn't sure what the atmosphere was going to be like at Brew's Clues, and I wanted to be prepared.

The keys in my hand jingle as I attempt to find the house keys. I really need to get a separate keychain for the shop. All of the ones I keep up with for Corey constantly get in the way of my own. With the correct one finally in my grasp, I slide it into the door knob at the same time arms wrapped around my waist. I must've been so focused on finding the right key that I didn't hear Adrian come up the steps. "You scared the crap out of me Adrian."

"Sorry. But it's not Adrian." I recognize the voice immediately, and fear shoots up my spine. No, this can't be *him*.

Spinning around, I'm confronted with the face of the last person I ever wanted to see again. I'm kicking myself for not paying attention to my surroundings like I promised my brother I would. Dawson looms before me, lips quirked up in a sadistic grin. "Hi Sophia, did you miss me?"

"Wh – what are you doing here?" The stutter in my words pisses me off, but I can't help it. Even after all this time Dawson is able to make me cower in fear. I can't let him see that, though. I need to be strong and brave.

"Don't be like that, baby." He pushes a piece of hair behind my ear and makes a face, disgusted. "I have to say; I'm not loving the new look."

I jerk away from him, my hands moving behind my back to get a grasp on the doorknob. If I'm fast enough I can fall inside and shut the door before he realizes what's happened. "You don't have a right to tell me what you do and don't like. Now, why are you here?" Hopefully my false bravado will turn into a real sense of fierceness and I can get him out of here without any help.

"Do you have any idea how hard it is to find you alone without your tattooed boyfriend?" Shit, he has been following me all this time. Now I wish I would have skipped book club and done something with Adrian instead. It would've only been a matter of time before he cornered me when I was alone, though. He's obviously been waiting for his opportunity.

"That still doesn't explain why you are here, Dawson." I can keep him talking, Adrian will be here soon and he can save me. As much as I don't want to be the girl that needs somebody to come to her rescue, right now I absolutely *need* it.

"Because," Dawson scowled. "It's the only way I can get you to talk to me. I've been waiting, biding my time until that stupid ass restraining order expired. When I saw I had my chance a few months ago, you walked out of that tattoo shop with some guy. And I couldn't approach you then."

He's getting angry and nothing good ever comes from that. He doesn't have anything to throw at me. Which is good and bad. There are other ways he can hurt me. I never thought I would long for the day when that would be the best-case scenario. His hands are balled into fists, and I need to do everything I can to keep them from being directed toward me. "Well," I take a deep breath. "You're here now, what do you want to talk about?"

His hands unfurl and I sigh in relief. "I want to get back together. We can work this out."

Seriously, that's what he wants to come at me with? It's been almost two years, and he hasn't gotten it through his head that we're over. "We aren't good together, Dawson."

"I've changed. I promise I have." He runs his hand down my arm pulling my own hand out from behind me. So much for trying to get inside. "We can give us another try."

Shaking my head, I look down at my feet. Please, Adrian, hurry up and get here. He leans his free arm against the wall over my head, caging me in so I have nowhere to go. "We aren't good for each other Dawson. Besides, I've moved on. I have a boyfriend now." Maybe placating him will help in letting him down easy. A car turns onto the small road my apartment is on, but it doesn't pull into a spot. And my hopes of it being Adrian die. I really need him to get here...soon.

Dawson's face turns bright red. That wasn't the right thing to say. "You left me, Sophia." He slams his hand against the wall, and grips my hand until pain shoots through my fingers. "I didn't even get a say in whether I wanted that outcome or not."

"This," I yell, trying to yank my hand out his hold. "This is why I left. Everything was your way or no way. You'd yell horrible things at me and hurl shit at me when

I did something that displeased you. Fuck Dawson, you are doing it *now* by showing up here and cornering me." I didn't mean to unleash on him but I've had enough. Let's hope my barbs don't cause him to act out.

He releases my hand, but brings his up, ready to strike a blow.

adrian

"GET your fucking hands off of her." A man has his fist raised in the air, moments away from letting it fall on the woman I love. This is the last thing I expected to see when I walked up the stairs to Sophia's apartment.

"Mind your own business," he says without even glancing my way.

I don't think, I only react. The bag holding our late-night pasta dinner and the flowers I picked up on the way over hit the concrete. Rushing toward him, I tackle him to the ground. Scraping my hands as they hit. "Who the hell do you think you are?"

"Adrian," Sophia shrieks my name. "He's not worth it." She's pulling at my arms begging me to get off this guy. "Dawson, you need to leave now."

This is that prick she lived with. Son of a bitch, I should have gone to book club with her tonight, or at least been here waiting for her when she got home. That would have prevented this asshole from approaching her. This time it's my fist in the air, and I swing. His lip is busted and my knuckles are covered in his blood. "What?" Dawson grins, blood coating his teeth. "You don't want your boy toy to know about me?"

"Don't you fucking talk to her, asshole." I punch him again. How dare he act as if she has been hiding him from me. "I know all about your worthless ass. You want to pick on someone and make them feel inadequate? You should do it to someone your own size."

He frees his arm from under me, and slams his fist into my ribs. "Is that better?" I roll off of him, grabbing my side. "You should have stayed out of this. It's between me and her," he points toward Sophia as he stands up, using the wall as support.

As for Sophia, tears are streaming down her face. She's staring at the scene before her, her hand covering her mouth, unmoving. "No." I stand up on shaky legs. Fuck my ribs hurt. Hopefully he didn't break any of them. "That ended when she walked out on you for being an abusive asshole."

"Is everything okay out here?" Sophia's neighbor, an older gentleman we've never see due to our hours at the shop, steps outside. He looks pointedly at Dawson. "I think you need to get out of here before I call the cops."

"This isn't any of your concern," Dawson sneers. "Besides, if I go... he goes." He nods his head in my direction.

"That's not how this is going to work," her neighbor

leans against his door. "I've seen him here before. You," he jabs his fingers in Dawson's direction, "I've never seen you here. And it looks like this young lady doesn't want you around."

Dawson is smart enough to know when he needs to back down. "We'll continue this talk later, Sophia." He walks down the stairs without another word. Over my dead body. That ass wipe isn't coming anywhere near my girl ever again.

"I'm Joe," he says, holding out his hand to me. "Are y'all okay?"

I shake his hand, and pull Sophia into my arms. Her head cheek rests against my chest, and she wraps her arms around my waist. "I'm fine, but I'm not sure what happened before I got here. I'm Adrian, by the way. And this," I gesture toward the woman in my arms, "is Sophia."

A sob tears itself from Sophia and her entire body is shaking against mine. Damn it, I should have been here. I pull her closer to me. "Did he hurt you?"

"Not really," she hiccups. "He squeezed my hand, and it hurts."

I grab her hand, inspecting it. It's red and will probably bruise. "We need to go to the cops. This should be enough to get that restraining order put back in place."

"I hope so," she breathes loudly, trying to get her crying under control. "Will you stay with me for the rest of the week?"

"Absolutely," I kiss the top of her head not wanting to

push her boundaries after dealing with her ex. I turn the key hanging out of her apartment door. "Can you wait here for a second, Joe? I'm going to get Sophia inside."

"Sure thing," he nods at me.

I gently nudge Sophia into her apartment, closing the door behind us. She stumbles and sinks to the floor. She looks so small right now. It kills me seeing her like this and not knowing what to do to make her feel better. To give her the sense of security she once had.

I place my arms underneath her knees and neck, and pick her up. If she can't carry the weight of her frustration and sadness, I'll do it for her. She is limp in my arms, all the fight drained out of her. And quite possibly in shock from the encounter. I walk over to the couch and sit down with her in my lap. I don't want to let her go and I need to feel her in my arms probably more than she wants to be in them. She's okay and that's what is important.

One of her favorite blankets is sitting on the back of the couch. I pull it down and wrap it around her, trying to put an end to her shaking body. "Sophia, baby, did he hurt you anywhere else besides your hand?"

She shakes her head but doesn't say anything else. Burying her face in my chest she begins sobbing. "Y– you came," the words come out in jagged breaths, "I was beginning to think you weren't going to show up at all. I tried to keep him calm and talking until you got here, but it didn't work. All I managed to do was antagonize him to the point he wanted to physically hurt me."

"I'm so sorry, Sophia. I was picking up things to make tonight special, or I would have been here much earlier. And this never would've happened. None of what happened tonight is your fault." Her tears leave wet paths down my shirt and I wish she never had a reason to cry. "He's the one that has problems, and if he was a real man, he wouldn't have let himself get so out of control.

"You're here," she clutches my shirt in her fist. "And that's all that matters. You are what I need to erase being in his presence."

"That's good," I chuckle trying to lighten the mood, or at least make her smile. "Because I am now your new accessory. Where you go, I go. I will not let him hurt you again." The corners of her lips lift up the tiniest fraction, and I know I've done my job. "In all seriousness, though. We need to go to the police station."

Her voice is barely above a whisper, "I know. Maybe this time they will grant me a restraining order."

"That's the goal." I slide out from under her until her body takes up the entire couch. Bending down until we're face-to-face, I meet her eyes. "I will be right back. I'm going to clean up our dinner off the patio, and ask your neighbor a few things. Are you going to be okay by yourself for a few minutes?"

"Yeah," she blinks. "I'm just going to close my eyes for a little bit." Her eyes drift shut, and I stay by her side until her breathing evens out. Pushing away the hair that is falling into her face I kiss her temple before getting up.

She's finally calming down, and at peace. At least until we have to the police.

Now that Dawson is no longer here, the night is still and serene. Joe has a small trash bag in his hand and he's bent over mine and Sophia's ruined dinner. "You didn't have to do that. I was on my way out here to take care of the mess."

"It's okay, Son," Joe says and nods at the door. "She needed you more than this needed to be picked up. Is everything okay now?"

"For now," I shrug. "We have to go to the police station so she can file a report." I scratch the back of my head, "Is there any chance you would be willing to be a witness in case we need one?"

"Absolutely," Joe nods. I bend down to help him with the rest of the trash. "Jackasses like that deserve whatever they have coming to them."

"Thank you," I gather up the crushed petals that fell off the flowers I brought Sophia. "I just need your name and phone number in case they want it."

"Will do," he pauses and leans back. "It's a good thing you got here when you did. I was about to come out myself. At first, I thought it was you, but then I heard shouting and knew it couldn't be."

"I didn't realize you knew what I looked like since we come in at such odd hours." I knew she had a neighbor; we've just never seen them. Or, at least I haven't. The lights are always dark in the apartment next door.

"I'm a night owl," he stands, knees popping during

the whole process. "I pay attention to what's happening on this side of the complex. It gives an old man like me something to do after retirement." He grabs the trash bag and opens his door. "I'll keep an eye out for that trouble maker from now on. Any sign of him and I'll call the cops."

"Thank you, Sir," I shake his hand. "I really appreciate it."

"No problem," he replies. "Just knock on the door when you head to the station, and I'll give you my information."

Sophia's uninjured hand is in mine. Her grip is strong enough that it's almost painful for me. An image of her in labor with my child one day, our hands a mirror of this but under better circumstances. I shake the thought away. It's too soon to think about that, but the fact I am has to mean something. I never envisioned Miranda in my future, and I can't think of one without Sophia in it.

Police stations aren't my favorite buildings. They are full of despair and dim lighting. This one is no different. We're sitting inside one of the conference rooms, waiting on the officer Sophia talked to when she suspected Dawson might be following her again.

"Are you ready to do this?" I whisper. It seems wrong to speak too loudly in here. Or, I could be paranoid. I feel like we're being watched from all sides.

"Yes," she sighs. "It'll be a relief to get this taken care of. I'll never miss a court date again, that's for sure." This girl is so much stronger than she realizes. Most women would stay in toxic relationships. Too scared to leave, but she *did* it. She left him and she handled herself well tonight when he showed up behind her.

A part of me worried she was seeing someone else, and I was ready to lose my temper. I'm glad I waited to see what was going on. I would have felt horrible if I left and something worse would have happened. Officer Daniels finally walks into the room. "Good evening, Sophia. What can I help you with tonight?"

She sets the hand Dawson had in his grip on the table. The redness has faded, but it's swollen and bruising is starting to show up around her fingers and wrist. "Is this enough to get a restraining order taken out on him?"

"When did this happen?" Daniels sits down next to Sophia and inspects her injury.

"Tonight," she answers, head lowered. She better not be ashamed. None of this is her fault, and I don't know what I can do to make her see that. "He showed up at my apartment. We got into an argument and he squeezed my hand so tight that he bruised it. He would have hit me if Adrian hadn't showed up." Finally, she looks at me with a sad smile. "Thank you, again."

I lean my forehead against hers. "I would do anything for you. The punch to the ribs was totally worth it."

"Wait," Officer Daniels puts his hand up. "You were in an altercation with her ex-boyfriend?"

"Yes," I nod. "It didn't last long, though. Sophia's neighbor stepped out before too much damage could be done. I have his name and phone number right here if you need to talk to him."

"That's helpful," he says and turns his attention back to Sophia. "I'll rush this and get a temporary order started for you." He stands up to leave the room. "I'll be back in just a moment to get your full statement. I want to get this paperwork started. I'm sorry I couldn't do more when you came to me the first time."

"I understand," Sophia says. "You are just doing your job. But thank you for getting the temporary order started."

"You're welcome." And just like that he's out of the room. I'm uncertain how long it's going to take but I'm happy they are listening this time. I send a quick text to Sophia's parents letting them know what's going on. All that's left to do is wait.

* * *

The sun is breaking over the horizon as we pull into the parking area for my apartment. It took hours for Sophia to give her statement to the police. They had her repeat it over and over again, making sure she didn't leave out any details. They also asked me if I wanted to press charges.

Since I threw the first punch, I thought it was best not to do anything.

"We're here," I shake her awake. We would have been here two hours ago, but Tom and Lisa rushed to the station and wanted to get an insanely early breakfast. I think they wanted to see that she was okay with their own eyes. I can't imagine being a parent and constantly worrying about the safety of my child.

"Okay," she opens the car door, and loses her footing in her sleepy state. I hurry around and scoop her into my arms. I'm not complaining, though. I'll carry her all the time if I have to. "Thank you for everything tonight. And for bringing me to your place. I know it's stupid, but I didn't feel safe going to my apartment," she leans her head against my shoulder, "not today anyway."

"There's no need to thank me, baby. I'd be a shitty boyfriend if I had done any different." Hell, I'd be a horrible human being if I had just walked away. It still baffles my mind that Joe is the only person that came out to see what the hell was going on. I need to buy him some sort of gift to show him how grateful I am for his interference.

I'm going to have to rethink the floor I live on. It's not a problem going up the stairs by myself. But I have a sleeping Sophia in my arms and it makes the trek more difficult. The halls are narrow and I'm walking at an awkward angle to keep from accidentally hitting her head on the wall.

I gently tickle her side to wake her again. "I need to set you down so I can unlock the door."

"Sure," she stands and leans against the wall. My girl hasn't had much rest tonight and I feel awful for waking her up so much.

Once we're inside, I lock the door behind us. Her steps are sluggish as we make our way to my bedroom. I pull back the covers and help her slide in. "I'm going to text Corey and let him know we won't be in until later this evening."

"No, we can go in at our normal time," she argues.

"That's not going to happen," I say as I shoot off a text to our boss. "You'll be lucky if he lets you come in at all." He responds within in seconds. Yep, we're both off for the rest of the day. I'm not telling her that, though. She'll protest until she's blue in the face. I'll just "forget" to wake her up.

I take off my jeans and shirt before sliding in behind her. My arms around her would be amazing, but I don't want her to feel smothered. I never want her to think of me in the same light as Dawson. My worry is unfounded, though. "Can you hold me?" Her voice is a whisper in the quiet room.

I wrap my arms around her, pulling her closer to me. There's no way in hell I'm ever letting this woman go.

IT FEELS great to be working again. Corey gave me a few days off to clear my head and take any precautions I felt I needed. Let's just say there are now cameras on my side of the patio. Mom and Dad have been helping out a lot. Jay tried to duck out of his classes and come down, but my parents threatened to make him stay home the rest of the semester if he did. He made the right decision by staying put. As much as he loves being home, he loves having freedom from our meddling parents.

"You holding up okay?" Bianca asks as she walks through the door. "Adrian filled us in on what happened. You did good, girl. Most people would have cowered in that situation." She holds her fist out to me, waiting for me to bump it. "You, my friend, are a badass."

She doesn't give me a chance to respond before she heads off to her workstation. That girl is something else, and I'm happy to have her as a friend. I have no doubt she would have handled things differently than me.

Adrian is holed up in his work room with the door closed. He only ever does that when he needs his full concentration and no interruptions. Whatever he's working on must be important, or very intricate. I can't wait to see the finished product, and know it will be amazing.

"How are the appointments looking today, Soph?" Where the hell did Charleigh even come from? I didn't hear her come in and she's never here before everyone else.

"Let me feel your forehead," I place my hand on her head, acting as if she's sick. "You are never here early. What gives?"

She shrugs, as if it's no big deal. "Someone had to fill in for you while you were gone. And since I'm the one who did it all before you, Corey nominated me to do it." She's pulling her long hair into a messy bun. "The only plus side is I beat Jake to the cereal. No more losing out on my favorite now."

"You are a mess," I laugh. "Why not just buy two boxes? That should fix things." It seems like the simplest solution to me anyway.

"It's the principle of the matter," she huffs. "I'm going to force myself to like all the things he likes so he feels the disappointment of his favorite foods being gone."

I don't see that ending well, but knowing Jake... he

probably does it to get a rise out of her. He's always done his best to push her buttons, wanting to know what's going to make her tick. "Good luck with that," I roll my eyes. "As far as appointments, it's a slow day for everyone."

"That's good," she nods, a wry smile crossing her lips before she schools her features. "You may want to go through the books and make sure Corey didn't screw anything up. You know how bad he is at keeping up with your system."

"Will do," I nod. "It's not like he needs a degree for it." I pull out the appointment book and slips of paper fall to the floor. Groaning, I pick them up. It's going to be a long day sorting through this mess.

"Sophia," Adrian calls my name. "Can you come here?"

The lobby is empty, and I've finally finished going through the mess Corey left me. One day I'm going to sit him down and show him how everything needs to be done.

Instead of responding I rush to the room. I haven't seen Adrian all afternoon, and I'm having withdrawals. "What's up?" I ask, opening the door.

He slides something under his notebook, hiding it before I have a chance to see what it is. "How much do you trust me?"

"This sounds like a loaded question," I cross my arms

over my chest. Adrian's eyes move down until he's star-ing. Uncrossing my arms, I move them to my hips instead. "Staring at my boobs isn't very professional."

"Neither is dating my co-worker, but I don't hear you complaining." He smiles wide. "Now, how much do you trust me?"

"Completely," I say, meaning it. If it wasn't for him there's no telling what would have happened to me the night Dawson showed up at my apartment. "Why?"

"I designed a tattoo for you."

I cut him off right there. "It's not something ridicu-lous like the one Charleigh inked onto Jake is it? Because I'm not sure how well I could pull off a cartoon character."

"No, it's not anything like that," he sighs. "It's special, and I want it to be a surprise."

"Okay, I'm down." Adrian is the only person who has not put ink on my skin, and even if this is a huge mistake, I'd love nothing more than for him to create his art on my body.

"Wow," he chuckles. "I expected more of a fight from you."

Shrugging, I take a step toward him. "I trust you not to make me look like a dumbass. Where do I need to sit?"

"Close the door," he nods toward it. "I need you to take your shirt off." When I give him a pointed look, he adds, "Your sleeve will get in my way."

I close the door, and take a seat in the chair across from him. He readies all of his supplies and pulls out the paper hidden beneath the notebook. "It's going to work out perfectly."

"I hope so," I mutter under my breath.

"It is. Stop freaking out." He rubs the transfer on my shoulder, and lets out a slow whistle. "Sit back and relax. This is my way of showing you how amazing you are."

"Fine," leaning my head back I close my eyes, waiting for the buzz of the tattoo gun to fill the room.

His touch is gentle, and I wasn't expecting that. I figured his strokes would be hard and precise, but I almost can't feel the needle piercing my skin. He goes in back and forth motions, and I close my eyes, basking in the closeness I feel with him. He's become my protector, friend, and boyfriend in such a short amount of time. If anyone would have told me that Adrian would be the person I turn to the most, three months ago, I wouldn't have believed them. Yet here we are, figuring out this murky thing they call love one step at a time.

I must have dozed off at some point because the room is quiet again. All of Adrian's supplies are put away, and he's wiping the last of the excess ink off of my skin. "Are you ready to see it?"

I jump out of the chair and run to the mirror. My jaw drops at the image he's created for me. An anchor takes up my entire shoulder. Strength written down the middle. The words "be your own anchor" in script beneath. "It's amazing, Adrian. I love it."

"I know you feel like you were weak the night *he* confronted you, but you aren't. I wanted to give you a small reminder of how strong you really are. Even if I'm not around, you have the strength to take care of yourself. You just have to dig deep enough within you to find it." He wipes wetness away from my cheeks. "Why are you crying?"

"Because it's beautiful, Adrian," I hiccup. "Not just the tattoo but everything you just said. You give me strength in ways you don't even realize. You are my home, and I don't want to go a day without you in my life. You saved me, literally and metaphorically. I swore dating off, and then you happened. You approached me when I was too scared to say anything to you. I love you so damn much." I wrap my arms around his neck and kiss him. I pour all of myself into that one simple action. My hopes, dreams and fears. Everything I want for us, for our future.

"I love you, too," his lips move against mine, "you are it for me."

"I better be," I laugh, pulling back, "I need to get back to work"

"Or you could stay in here the rest of the day," he wriggles his eyebrows.

"Nope," I shake my head. "I haven't been here in days. If I give all of you a break, you'll think you can run all over me."

Opening the door, I walk to my desk in the lobby. A year ago, I wouldn't have thought this possible. When I walked into Life in Ink to get my first tattoo, I wasn't looking for anything more than a reminder that I'm enough. I've gained so much more. A group of friends that is more like family, and an amazing guy who will literally take a punch to protect me. Even though there will be adjustments and difficulties as I face Dawson in court, I know I'll be okay. I have Adrian by my side, and I can always count on him to lift me up. To show me that I'm strong and he loves me without any strings attached.

Turn the page to read the first chapter of Gone Country, the first book in the upcoming Cousins Gone RomCom series.

Stella

There's a soft knock on my office door. It opens slowly, and Ellen pokes her head inside. "Stella, Mr. Hart wants you in his office as soon as possible." She closes the door before I have a chance to respond, and scurries away to her desk.

This is one of the things I loathe about working at this company. I have busted my ass to get where I am, but I'm expected to drop everything to meet the demands of others. If I wasn't scared I'd be fired, I wouldn't even bother going to see what Mr. Hart wants. Alas, here I am pushing my chair back and running off the moment they have summoned me.

My heels click clack against the hard floor, earning me curious glances from the customer service employees in the main area. There are usually only two reasons a person is called into the owner's office... You are either being promoted or let go. Worry gnaws at my gut at the prospect of being fired. I just bought a new house and car after spending years saving, and I can't afford to no longer have a job.

Mr. Hart's personal secretary is seated at her desk in front of his office. "Hi Rosie, how are you doing today?"

"Oh, just fine." Her slightly wrinkled hand picks up the cup of coffee sitting in front of her and she takes a sip. She's much older then she looks, but I guess all the beauty products she's had sent here over the years have helped stop the aging process. I only hope to look as great as she does when I'm her age. That's a life goal, right there.

"That's great," I smile. "Um, Mr. Hart asked speak with me?" Nerves are the only thing I can blame for making that statement come out as a question. Now is not the time for them to shake me up.

Rosie waves toward the door, "Go on in, Dear. He's waiting for you."

"Thanks Rosie," I give her desk a quick tap. Swallowing down my nerves, I knock on Mr. Hart's door twice even though it's open, and step inside. It's time to face whatever is awaiting me inside.

"Oh, Stella, you're here." Mr. Hart is looking at me through his thick wire-rimmed glasses. Honestly, glasses like that should have a plastic frame, but I'm not going to be the one to tell him that. "Come on in, and have a seat."

I hurry over to the chair closest to his desk. To most

people the seat they choose to sit in wouldn't be a big deal, except it is to me. The chair closest to him shows that I'm not afraid of him, even though I'm terrified of what he could potentially say. "You asked to see me?"

He sets the pen and the paper pad he was writing on aside, and meets my gaze. "Yes, I have an opportunity I would like to discuss with you."

A sigh of relief escapes my body without my permission, and I wish I could take it back. It shows a sign of weakness, and that's never a good thing when it comes to women in this male-dominated industry. "What did you have in mind, Sir?"

"We are opening up a new distribution center outside of a small town in North Texas." He leans closer as if readying himself to tell me a secret. "As head of operations management, I want you to relocate there until the job is complete, and it's running smoothly."

The excitement I had at the word opportunity dies with the word relocation. I love living in Austin, and moving to a small town, even for a little bit, is not in my plan. "Are you sure I'm the right fit for this job?" Probably not the best question to follow up with, but I *really* don't want to move to a small town. I spent my entire life trying to get out of one.

He must see that I'm not bouncing with joy to go. "Yes, you are. You aren't afraid to make the hard decisions and get things done." He leans back in his chair, and almost falls backwards. Correcting himself and placing his hand over his protruding stomach, he adds,

"Did I mention we are also going to pay for the house you'll be staying in, and it comes with a healthy bonus."

That is almost enough to make me consider the offer. If it means more money in my bank account, and a possible promotion, then I'm one hundred percent in. "How healthy are we talking?"

acknowledgments

This is the last book in the Taking Chances series, and it's bittersweet. I loved writing each and every one of these characters, even when they pissed me off. It's hard telling them goodbye, but I'm excited to start working on another series. There may be a few surprise guests...

There are so many people to thank. My parents for their continued support of my dreams, listening to my business talk, and offering ideas on what I should do.

Hubs, Boy Child, and Wee One, I can't thank you enough. Y'all are my inspiration every day. I do what I do because the three of you believe in me. You understand my late night writing sessions, and get as excited as I do when I release another book. I love y'all to the moon and back.

My besties Nessa, Cindy, Kelsie & Tasha, you make my days better. I can't imagine a world where all of you aren't a part of my life. I love you ladies something fierce.

My team, Small Edits, KP Designs, and Aurora... Y'all make doing what I do a breeze. From the quick edits, to the covers that nail the mood every time, and the last minute requests to make an image or form, you three always have my back. Thank you all so much.

Dreamers, I can't even tell y'all how much y'all mean to me. I love jumping in our group and talking about random things. Movie nights and book club discussions are always a blast as well. Y'all freaking rock!

Last, but definitely not least, readers and bloggers. Thank you for picking up my books and reading them. Seeing you connect with my characters is one of the best feelings ever. Keep being awesome readers!

also by katrina marie

The Taking Chances Series

Welcome to Your Life

Cruel and Beautiful World

Ways to Go

Remember That Night

My Only Wish is You

From This Moment

Shoot Down the Stars

Love Will Save Your Soul

Gone in Love Series

Out of the Ashes Series

Cocky Hero Club

Big Baller

Silverwood Bulldog Series

Baseball & Broadway

Katrina Marie lives in the Dallas area with her husband, two children, and fur baby. She is a lover of all things geeky and Gryffindor for life. When she's not writing you can find her at her children's sporting events, or curled up reading a book.
Visit her online: katrinamarieauthor.com
Sign up for my newsletter for extras from Welcome to Your Life: http://bit.ly/2BlDSsZ

facebook.com/KatrinaMarieAuthor
twitter.com/katrmarieauthor
instagram.com/katrinamarieauthor
bookbub.com/profile/katrina-marie
amazon.com/Katrina-Marie/e/B0749SZVTK/ref=dp_byline_cont_ebooks_1

www.ingramcontent.com/pod-product-compliance
Lightning Source LLC
Chambersburg PA
CBHW061817190726
48289CB00007B/2223